Miss Frost Saves the Sandman

A Nocturne Falls Mystery
Jayne Frost, book three

KRISTEN PAINTER

Dedicated to all of us
who never seem to get enough sleep.

Welcome to Nocturne Falls, the town that celebrates Halloween 365 days a year.

Jayne Frost is a lot of things. Winter elf, Jack Frost's daughter, Santa Claus's niece, heir to the Winter Throne and now…private investigator. Sort of.

When the Sandman comes to Santa's Workshop, the shop Jayne manages, to do his first ever book signing, it's a major event. He's kind of a supernatural celebrity and she needs to keep him happy.

All is well until trouble shows up at the party thrown in his honor. Trouble in the form of Luna Nyx, the Mistress of Nightmares and his creepy counterpart. The Sandman's assistant says Luna is dangerous, and Jayne believes it when her dreams turn dark.

Can Jayne keep the Sandman safe from this gothic goddess? Or will Luna's threats put them both to sleep for good?

MISS FROST SAVES THE SANDMAN:
A Nocturne Falls Mystery
Jayne Frost, Book Three

ISBN: 978-1-941695-23-4

Want to know when Kristen's next book is coming out? Join her mailing list for release news, fun giveaways, insider scoop and more!
NEWSLETTER
http://bit.ly/1kkLgH

Tempus Sanders, aka the Sandman (yes, *the* Sandman) was the biggest elf I'd ever seen. Actually, he was the biggest *anything* I'd ever seen.

I wasn't sure how tall he was, or how wide, but standing beside him in the warehouse of Santa's Workshop made me feel like a delicate flower. Which is not a description ever really used about me, even though I am the Winter Princess.

Despite his size, Tempus wasn't intimidating, probably because his body shape more closely resembled a marshmallow Peep more than anything else. If I'm being perfectly honest, he was kind of a little blobby. But in a good way. It was comforting somehow. Like a giant stuffed animal you could just cuddle up with and...well...sleep.

Which made sense, seeing as how sleep was his kingdom.

Sleep was also the reason he was here at my store. The Sandman had written a children's book guaranteed to put kids to sleep. There was no way *Hush,*

Little Baby wouldn't be a hit once parents figured out what it could do, but to make sure the book had the best launch possible, my dad, Jack Frost, and my uncle, Kris Kringle, had decided that the Santa's Workshop store in Nocturne Falls (the location I managed) should be the site of the event.

We ran the stores as a way to test out all the new toys my uncle's tinkers invented. And sure, to make money. Running a magical Christmas wonderland like the North Pole took some ice. But having the book launch at my store was pretty awesome. I knew they also thought that if anything supernatural happened, Nocturne Falls would be the place least likely to get bent out of shape about it.

They were right. This town could handle just about anything. But I'd been the manager of this shop less than a year, so the question really was, could I handle it? I certainly hoped so.

After all, the Sandman wasn't just physically big, he was a supernatural celebrity. A paranormal paragon. A magical rockstar. You get the picture.

Anyway, with his marshmallow body and his deep, melodic voice, it was no wonder he was the King of Dreams. Just being around him made me want to nap.

His assistant, on the other hand, was a hummingbird on crack. A humorless, uber-efficient hummingbird on crack. Without all the pretty hummingbird colors.

Olive Pine stood at Sanders' side, notepad at the ready. Her hair was scraped back into a ponytail so tight her brows seemed permanently suspended an inch above the rims of her glasses. Based on the color of her hair (so blue it was almost black), I knew she had talent when it came to magical abilities, but her real skills seemed to lie in her ability to keep Sanders on track.

She pushed her frames back on her nose to stare at me. "Mr. Sanders should be getting to his room. He needs to settle in and get ready. Tomorrow's a big day. Big day." She tapped her pen on the notepad. "He wants to be in the store as soon as it opens. And the store opens at—"

"Olive, I assure you, I know when the store opens." I smiled, trying to be patient. "I'm the manager, after all."

"Yes, you are. I have that in my notes. Jayne Frost, store manager. And Winter Princess." Her mouth formed a little knot that made her expression rather pensive. Like she was waiting for something to happen but wasn't sure what.

"That's me." I almost felt sorry for her. She'd probably done more work than any of us getting ready for this event. "I promise I'll take you up to the visitor's suite just as soon as he's done looking around."

Sanders had never been to one of the company stores before and had wanted a tour of the warehouse. I couldn't blame him—it was one of my favorite places. Dim and cool and cavernous. It felt peaceful to me. Sort of like my very own Fortress of Solitude.

He walked down the center aisle toward us, his warm brown eyes glittering. "I like this place."

In the large space, his deep voice set off a small

echo. I returned his grin. "Me, too. And not just because I work here." I pointed to the rooms behind me. "That's my office, and the door next to it goes into the employee breakroom."

He nodded, coming to a stop next to us. I had to tip my head back to keep eye contact. He put his enormous hands on his hips and took one more look around. "Your father and uncle know what they're doing, don't they?"

"Yes, sir, they do." I glanced at Olive, who was studying her watch. "Ready to go up to your rooms?"

He nodded. "Lead the way."

I took them to the elevator, slightly concerned Sanders might not fit. He had to duck, but then fit okay. Okay being a relative word. Olive and I were a little squished. Thankfully, Kip, one of the shop employees, had already taken Sanders' luggage up. I'd asked Kip to do it, but he'd been so excited about meeting Sanders that I got the feeling he would have volunteered anyway.

We got off on the third floor and I walked them to the guest suite. The apartments on this floor were bigger than the ones on the second floor where I lived. I could have had one of these—the previous manager's apartment, actually—but I'd already settled into my apartment downstairs. And how much room did one person need anyway?

It was just me and Spider, my cat. My *talking* cat. But I didn't really mention that to anyone anymore because I was the only one he ever spoke in front of. Apparently, that's how the magic that had given him that ability worked.

I unlocked the door, opened it, then handed Sanders the key ring, which held the apartment key and the key to the warehouse door. I had a copy of all the keys in my office. "Here you go. I hope it's to your liking."

"It looks very good." He took the keys, then handed them to Olive before entering the apartment.

She followed him, tucking the keys into the messenger bag slung across her body.

I came in behind them and shut the door. "The layout's pretty easy. Two bedrooms, two bathrooms with an open kitchen, dining and living room area. You need anything at all, just ask."

He nodded, doing a slow three-sixty. "Very nice." He faced me. "There is one thing. I could use something to eat."

I bet he could. How many calories did it take to fuel a body that size? "The kitchen is stocked with a variety of things, including selections from one of the best sweet shops in town." Three boxes' worth, actually. When Delaney Ellingham had heard who was coming to launch his new book at my shop, she'd gone a little overboard, insisting on packing the boxes herself. I'd thought being a new mom would slow her down a little, but that didn't seem to be the case.

The Ellinghams had also decided to throw a party in Sanders' honor, which meant tomorrow night after the shop closed, we were all headed to Elenora Ellingham's estate for a black tie affair. My dad and uncle had thought it was a great idea so I'd had my mom send some of my fancy stuff through the Santa's Bag, the transfer system that magically allowed us to send things between the store and the North Pole.

Being a princess meant I had a lot to choose from. No need to buy something new. And after stocking up on flip-flops and shorts to combat the summer heat in Georgia, wearing a formal gown was going to be an interesting change of pace.

It was worth it, though, to meet the grand dame of the Ellingham clan and get a look inside her place. I'd been by it a few times and from the outside, it was majorly impressive. Plus I'd heard no one threw a party like Elenora, and after deciding not to attend the recent Black and Orange Halloween Ball, I was almost looking forward to this.

But back to Sanders and his dietary requirements.

"I'd be happy to order you something. Do you like pizza? There's a phenomenal pizza place in town. Salvatore's. Really good pies."

He squinted as if in thought. "Pizza sounds great."

"Sure. What do you like on yours?"

"Everything," Olive answered before he could say a word. "But peppers."

Sanders laughed and put his hand on his stomach. "Yes, peppers and I are not friends."

"Great, I'll get right on that." I pulled out my cell phone. "How many would you like?"

"Six. Large." He pointed at his assistant. "And whatever Olive would like."

I tried not to react to the size of his order. "Okay." I looked at Olive. "What can I get you?"

"Small, plain cheese pizza."

"That's it?"

She answered without looking up from scribbling something in her notepad. "Yes."

"Got it." I hit the button for Salvatore's and placed my order, which had to be the biggest I'd ever given them. When I was done, I hung up and spoke to Sanders, who'd gotten himself a soda from the fridge and was wandering around the living room like he was ready to relax. I could take a hint. "I'll bring the pizzas up when they arrive, but for now I'll let you get settled in."

"Thank you, Jayne. You're an excellent hostess."

I smiled. "Thank you. See you in about half an hour."

I took the stairs to the floor below and headed straight to Juniper's apartment. Juni had become one of my best friends, along with Buttercup, the slightly Goth girl who was the evening shift manager. Besides the two of them, the other store employees were Holly and Kip, the two who'd arrived not long after I had, and the newest employee, Rowley Gladstone.

Rowley was a retired tinker like the manager I'd replaced, but my father assured me the older man had no aspirational dreams beyond working in the store now that he'd retired. He'd moved here with his wife, Dorthea. She was also retired, having worked in one of the company's cafeterias as a baker. That was a big gold star as far as I was concerned. And Rowley was a fast, eager learner, already handling things in the shop like a pro despite only being here a week. For as well as I knew him and his wife, I liked them both.

I knocked on Juni's door. Buttercup answered. "Hey. You get Sanders settled in?"

"I did."

Juni showed up a second later with a plate of

7

cookies in her hand. "Did he like the apartment?"

"Seemed to. I just ordered them some pizzas. You guys want to help me deliver them?"

"Do you really need help or is this just so I can meet him?" Buttercup asked. She'd been working in the store so hadn't gotten the chance yet.

"I need the help. There are seven pies coming."

"Wow, he's an eater, huh?" She grinned. "Sure, I'm in. I can't wait to meet him."

"Cool."

Juni nodded too. "Happy to help. You want to come in and taste this new batch of shortbread while we wait? It's Dorthea's recipe."

"Did you really need to ask?" I shut the door behind me and helped myself to a cookie. It crumbled into buttery goodness on my tongue. "Mmm, these are great. Does Delaney know you're cutting into her sales?"

Juniper laughed. "Fortunately for her, my baking is just a hobby. It's Dorthea she needs to watch out for. Hey, do you think I should take some of these up to Mr. Sanders?"

"He'd love them. Or you could keep them all here and give them to me." I smiled hopefully.

She snorted. "I could, but I don't think you can assure me of pleasant dreams." She took the plate into the kitchen and got out the cling wrap. "Off to our celebrity guest, then."

Buttercup and I settled onto the couch. A Reese Witherspoon movie was playing on the TV but the sound was turned down.

Buttercup faced me, tucking one leg underneath

the other. Her galaxy print leggings and black T-shirt looked very comfy. "Juniper said Sanders' assistant is a real piece of work."

Juniper joined us, taking the side chair. The plate of cookies had been tragically left behind on the counter. "Yeah, what's her name? Something like pickle. I know that's not it but that's all I can remember."

"Olive," I corrected. "Olive Pine."

Buttercup sucked in a breath. "Olive Pine is the Sandman's assistant?"

"Yep. You know her?"

Buttercup shrugged. "We went to school together, but I didn't know her very well. I don't think anyone did. We were in the same graduating class. But she kept to herself. Especially after the incident."

"The incident?" I leaned back. "Wait, was she as tightly wound then as she is now?"

Buttercup raised her eyebrows. "She was voted most likely to run the North Pole Statistics Department before she was thirty."

"Sounds like she hasn't changed."

"Yeah, well, we weren't sure she'd end up getting employment after what she did senior year."

Juniper's eyes widened. "Is that 'the incident'? What did she do?"

With obvious relish, Buttercup wiggled further back on the couch. "Well, I'm not one to gossip, but this is a true story so…" She cleared her throat. "Olive broke into the school office and changed the grades of her crush, Lyle Bell. He was the captain of the curling team and a major babe. If you like jocks." She made a face like she didn't see the appeal. "Anyway, Olive only got caught because a janitor saw her leaving the building after hours."

I shook my head. "Why did she change his grades? If he was on the curling team, they would had to have been pretty decent already."

"They were. But not decent enough for him to get into Olive's top pick college. She confessed to hoping the bump in GPA would make it possible for them to attend the same school."

"And what did her boyfriend think of all this?" Juniper asked.

"Oh, Lyle wasn't her boyfriend. Olive wanted him to be, but so did ninety percent of the rest of the school. He claimed to be flattered by it, but insisted he knew nothing about it. I believed him. So did everyone else."

It seemed a little crazy to me. "What happened to Olive?"

Buttercup smirked. "She kind of snapped. She was so wound up about the guy that she ended up having to go to counseling for mental distress. Because of that, she got a slap on the wrist. It didn't even go on her permanent record. The next year she started college like nothing had ever happened."

"Huh." I shot Juniper a look. She seemed as stunned as I was. "I guess Lyle went to a different school."

Buttercup laughed. "Lyle moved to Sweden and tried out for the national curling team, who promptly made him an offer. I don't think he's been back to the North Pole since."

We sat in silence for a moment, light from the movie flickering behind us. Finally, I spoke. "Do you think Sanders knows? Not that it matters, I guess. I mean, that was high school. People do stupid things in the name of love all the time at that age."

"Yeah," Juniper said. "But I bet he knows. It might not have gone into her permanent record, but your dad runs a pretty tight ER department."

"True. Look what Elf Resources puts people through just to work here." Still, I couldn't help but wonder if that was something they would have passed on. "Well, it's not my business anyway. But wow, right?"

Juniper and Buttercup both nodded. "Right. Yep."

I checked the time on my phone. "Pizza should be here any second."

Buttercup put her hand on her stomach. "You should have ordered an extra one for us."

I grinned. "Who says I didn't?"

She fist-bumped me. "You're awesome."

I lifted one shoulder. "I know."

Juniper pointed at the door. "Did I just hear knocking?"

I jumped up. "I'll check."

Sure enough, the Salvatore's delivery guy stood at my door.

"Hey, Franklin. I'm over here." Yes, I ordered enough from them to be on a first name basis with the guys who brought the food.

He turned around. "Hi, Miss Frost. Big order tonight." He turned and handed the stack of boxes to me.

I promptly handed them off to Buttercup and Juniper, who stood at the ready. "Yep, company in town."

He pulled the receipt and a pen from his apron. "I just need you to sign this."

I took the receipt, added a generous tip and my signature, then handed it back. This was going on the company credit card. "Thanks, have a good night."

"You too. Enjoy." He waved and left.

"Which one is ours?" Buttercup asked.

"Half meat, half veggie. The rest go upstairs."

"Found it," Juniper said. She put that box aside.

"All right, let's deliver these, then we can eat." We each took a few boxes and trekked upstairs, by elevator since we were carrying precious cargo.

Sanders met us at the door. "Good evening, ladies."

"Your dinner has arrived," I announced.

"And in such style." He inhaled and smiled. "What could be better than pizza delivered by three gorgeous women? Come in, ladies, come in."

Even Buttercup smiled, which wasn't something she typically did around strangers. But being around Sanders had that affect.

We set the pizzas on the dining table, then I introduced the girls again. "You remember Juniper from earlier, I'm sure. And this is Buttercup. She's the evening shift manager."

"Of course, I remember Juniper." He extended his big hand to Buttercup. "And it's a pleasure to meet you, Buttercup. Thank you both for helping Jayne with the pizza. I wish you all happy dreams."

Juniper's eyes went a little blissful. I'm not sure what she'd been hoping for, but it seemed like she'd just gotten it.

"We'll let you and Olive eat." I looked around but didn't see her, which was odd since she'd been glued to him earlier. "I'll see you in the morning."

Just then, Olive walked out of the second bathroom, wrapped in a robe, a towel turban holding her hair. "Tempus, we should go over…" She stopped when she saw us, pulling the robe tighter. "I didn't hear you come in. I guess the pizza is here."

"It is," Buttercup said.

Olive paled a split second after her gaze landed on Buttercup's face. Then she cleared her throat and took a few steps backwards. "I should get dressed. If you'll excuse me." She disappeared into the second bedroom.

Sanders clasped his hands in front of him. "Thank you again, ladies."

"You're welcome." I herded Buttercup and Juniper out the door.

No one said a word until we were back in Juni's apartment.

Buttercup spoke first. "She definitely remembers me."

Juni nodded as she grabbed plates out of the cabinet. "Did you see the look on her face? Like she'd seen a ghost."

I took a plate and helped myself to a slice of veggie. "This could be weird."

Buttercup went for the meat. "Not on my end. If it's weird for her, that's her doing. I don't care what she did all those years ago."

"She's just embarrassed," Juniper said. "Caught off guard. Working with Sanders means she's been out of the Pole for a bit. She probably didn't think she'd run into anyone she knew."

I took my slice to the table. "I hope you're right."

Buttercup took the seat across from me. "I know you're on the line for this event. I promise, I'm not going to do anything to screw that up for you. I swear."

"Thanks." I nodded. "And I appreciate that, but you all have to be in the store together. I just hope Olive can let it go too."

Juniper put a jug of lemonade on the table along with three plastic cups. "And if she can't?"

I sighed and poured lemonade into the cups for all three of us. "Then I guess I have to be the manager and smooth things over."

I lifted my cup and they joined me. "To a successful event."

"Here, here," Juniper said.

Buttercup nodded. "Ditto."

We heard knocking as we finished making our toast.

"Sounds like your apartment." Buttercup bit the end off her pizza.

"Yep. Going to see." I got up, went to the door and opened it.

Olive Pine stood in front of my door.

"Hey, Olive. Over here."

"Oh!" Olive turned, a little flustered, perhaps because I hadn't shown up at the door she'd expected. She looked past me, but Buttercup and Juniper had stayed at the table. Olive's gaze stayed on them, so I took the cue and stepped into the hall, shutting the door behind me.

"Does Sanders need something?" But after the way she'd looked at Buttercup, I had a feeling I knew what was up.

She sighed and finally made eye contact with me. "No, he's fine. I...I just thought..." Another sigh. "Look, I'm going to be straight with you. I know Buttercup from school and before a story gets started, you should know that I had some difficulties in my past, but I'm well beyond that. The past really is the past. We all do dumb things when we're young, right?"

"Right." I smiled to reassure her and, for the first time, felt some sympathy for her. Behind the uptight, by-the-book exterior was a woman only a few years younger than me trying to make her way in the world. Sanders couldn't be an easy man to work for and I got the sense that Olive was doing her best to not only keep him happy, but rise above her past. "Whatever happened, happened. And I'm sure you've got your hands full with Sanders."

She smiled. "I do. But Tempus is a wonderful man and a joy to work for. I love my job. And I want this book launch to be as successful as it can be."

"So do I. Let's just move forward from here, okay?"

"Yes. Thank you. Would you mind speaking to Buttercup and asking her not to say anything to anyone about what happened? Granted, it's within her rights but it would be easier if it didn't come up."

"I'll take care of it."

Her shoulders dropped and she let out a breath. "I appreciate that."

"No problem. I'll see you and Sanders at nine a.m. then, and we'll go over the schedule for the signing one more time."

She nodded and started down the hall toward the elevator. "Nine sharp. Thank you again."

"You're welcome." I opened the door to go back to my friends and my pizza. It looked like Buttercup and Juniper were already on slice number two. I took my seat at the table and grabbed a second one so I could catch up.

"Everything cool?" Buttercup asked.

I ate a bite of lukewarm but still delicious pizza. "She recognized you and wanted to head off any doubts I might have about her based on her past."

"So she assumed I'd tell you?" Buttercup rolled her eyes.

I laughed as I put my pizza down to grab my drink. "Well, you did."

She shrugged. "True."

Juniper wiped her mouth. "What did she say?"

"That her past is just that—behind her. And I believe her. She seems to love her job and definitely wants to keep it, so I get it. She doesn't want something that happened years ago to mar her life now." I looked at Buttercup and Juniper. "No one else hears about the grade changing thing, okay?"

They both nodded and Juniper crossed her heart.

"Good." I picked up my slice again. "Now let's finish this pie before it gets any colder."

Juniper smiled. "Too bad Cooper's not around to warm it up."

"Speaking of Cooper," Buttercup started. "Who's taking you to the party tomorrow?"

I wrinkled my nose. They weren't going to like my answer. Which is why I hadn't told them yet. "Um...Cooper—"

"I knew it," Juniper said. "I knew you'd come to your senses."

"*And* Greyson," I finished.

Buttercup's mouth gaped open. "What? How did you swing that?"

"How could I not? How could I take one and not the other? I already went through this with the Halloween Ball. It's the reason I didn't go! And it wasn't like I could hide it from either one. Nor would

17

I want to."

Doubt clouded Juniper's eyes. "How is this going to work exactly?"

"Cooper is taking me and Greyson is bringing me home. They each get half of the evening."

Buttercup snorted. "And who's refereeing the time?"

"They've agreed to be cool about it." And that had better be the case. Not that I thought myself so special that these two amazing guys would be fighting over me, but men were men and things happened. In theory, they were mature enough to behave, but if they weren't, being at Elenora Ellingham's ought to reinforce the need for civility. Especially since they both technically worked for the town and the Ellinghams ran the place.

"Can't wait to see how that goes," Buttercup mumbled.

Me either, but I wasn't saying anything more about it. I shifted the conversation to the big book signing tomorrow and we finished our pizza while talking about it.

I helped clean up, then said good night and went back to my apartment. Tomorrow was a big day, and we had a lot to do so I was headed straight to bed.

After feeding Spider, of course. He was sitting by his food bowl. I guess in case I'd forgotten where it was.

"Hungry," he yowled.

I reached down and scooped him up, holding him like a baby and kissing his nose. "I know, you poor thing. You're just starving, aren't you? It's like I didn't even feed you three hours ago."

"Hungry." But this time it was more of a statement than a demand.

I put him down. His bowl was empty. "Chicken Party?" Because these days, he rarely ate anything else.

"Chicken Party," he answered enthusiastically.

I grabbed a can and his bowl and got to work. I was pretty used to having a talking cat now. So much so that it didn't seem weird to me at all any more. And since Spider had yet to talk in front of anyone but me, I didn't have to explain it, which made life simpler.

I dumped the pate into the bowl. His vocal prowess had happened accidentally a few months ago thanks to a wish granted by an imp, but this was Nocturne Falls. Weird was normal and strange was routine. I put his dish down in front of the petite velvet Elvis-as-a-cat painting I'd bought to decorate his dining area. "Here you go, dig in."

Spider went to town, making happy little noises as he ate.

I went to clean my face and brush my teeth. I had a feeling tonight was going to be one of those nights where I fell asleep instantly.

That didn't stop me from doing a little reading, though. And about five minutes after I was settled in with my e-reader propped on my stomach, Spider sauntered in. He jumped onto the bed and curled up against my side. The snoring started shortly after.

I laughed softly, and since I could feel sleep tugging at me, powered the e-reader down, turned the lights off and closed my eyes.

Juniper had been so sure Sanders was going to give us some kind of extra-special dreams that I couldn't wait to see what happened.

I woke up in a pitch-black room with sweat dripping off me and my heart pounding. I sat up, unable to shake the terror that had just had a hold of me. I'd dreamed that Spider had turned into an actual spider, trapped me in his web, and was coming to eat me. His fangs were enormous.

Okay, that sounded a little silly now. But my breathing was only starting to slow. It had been so real. So much for the Sandman's sweet dreams.

I reached out, feeling the warm weight of Spider near my hip. I gave him a scratch, more to reassure myself than anything. "You wouldn't eat Mama, would you, Spider-cat?"

He yawned, tightened into a ball and muttered, "Spider likes Chicken Party."

Apparently, it was a good thing I wasn't a tasty poultry pate. I shook my head, my nightmare fading. "Go back to sleep."

I lay down and took my own advice.

By morning, the nightmare was forgotten in the hustle of getting ready for the day. The signing didn't start until three, but Sanders had the reading first. That was at ten at the Nocturne Falls library. We figured that was a safe place for him to put the kids of town to sleep. And when the parents saw how well the book worked, they'd flock to the store this afternoon to purchase the book.

But I was meeting Sanders and Olive in my office to go over the day's schedule before the car service arrived to take us to the library, and I needed to be down there at nine.

That meant breakfast was a package of frosted cinnamon toaster pastries, a handful of gummy bears and a Dr Pepper. That might not seem like a healthy breakfast to most people, but winter elves needed their sugar.

It was doing a body good.

My standard work outfit was usually more casual, but today I'd opted for a pencil skirt, silk blouse, and low, sensible heels with my diamond stud earrings and the strand of pearls my aunt and uncle had given me for graduation (diamond clasp in the back). I pulled my hair back in a low pony, added some simple makeup and checked myself in the mirror. Classy and understated. Perfect for today. After all, I was not the star of this show.

Even if I was the Winter Princess.

I grabbed my purse, my phone and my keys and blew a kiss to Spider (who had two very full bowls of food to keep him going) as I headed out.

Juniper was already at the elevator. "Hey. You look spiffy."

"Thanks. How was your night?"

She grinned. "I had the most amazing dream. Unicorns, flying, cotton candy clouds...it was *beyond*. And I feel like I could run a marathon this morning. You?"

"Wow, that is super cool." I didn't want to tell her about the bad dream I'd had. She'd been so sure Sanders was going to give us all some kind of miraculous sleep that I didn't want to ruin it.

The elevator doors opened and we got on.

"It was. I can't wait to see what Buttercup dreamed about." She looked at me a little closer. "I don't think I've ever seen you look so...corporate."

I laughed. "I'm taking that as a compliment because that's what I was going for."

She grinned. "You really do look nice. And there's a little bit of that hot-for-teacher thing going on too."

"Hah! Too bad I'm not meeting one of the boys for lunch. I might have to put this outfit into rotation."

"Like they're not already interested in you enough."

The elevator stopped and we got out. Juniper went toward the shop door. "Have a good day at the library. I've got everything under control here."

"I know you do. And thanks. Oh, and don't forget Rowley's coming in at noon. Put him to work shelving those new robotic kits."

"Will do, boss." She shot me a finger gun.

I laughed and headed to my office, leaving the door open. I only had a few minutes before Sanders showed up. I straightened things up a bit, more a nervous thing than because my office was a mess—it wasn't. I worked hard to keep it tidy. I got my schedule out, laying it front and center on my desk, and went over the day once more.

Sanders walked in exactly at nine a.m. He was dressed pretty much as he had been last night, in a loose tunic and matching pants. Yesterday's had been toffee colored; today's were sky blue. The best way I could describe them was fancy daytime pajamas. I'm pretty sure it was his uniform and, given who he was, the outfit made sense.

But there was one thing different about him today. A length of silk cord traversed his hips like a sash and off that cord hung one of the most curious objects I'd ever seen: his gold hourglass. The crystal chambers top and bottom held tiny grains of gold, supposedly one for each person in the world, and with that hourglass he safeguarded and regulated the sleep of every person on the planet, human and supernatural alike.

The hourglass was generally considered one of the most magical objects in the known universe (along with my uncle's time-traveling sleigh and my dad's ice scepter). I had no idea how the thing's magic worked, but it was so pretty and shiny that I couldn't stop myself from staring.

Sanders laughed. "Morning, Miss Frost. I see you've spotted my hourglass."

I forced myself to make eye contact. "It's beautiful. And good morning! I'm sorry for staring, but it's hard not to."

He nodded and patted the hourglass. "I understand. Do you think I should leave it off for today? I just don't like to be parted from it."

"No, it's fine. It's who you are, after all. And the kids will love it."

Olive cleared her throat. "Speaking of the children, we'd like to get to the library a little earlier than scheduled. Just to make sure things are set up properly."

I had no doubt they were. The librarian I'd worked with to set the event up was a very smart woman and excited to host the event. Of course, Miriam Newburg thought that Tempus Sanders was coming *dressed* as the Sandman, not that he actually *was* the Sandman, but she was human so allowances had to be made.

Whatever. I wasn't going to argue with Olive. "That's fine. I'll call the car service and see if they can be here sooner."

She checked something off on her notepad. "Thank you."

The buzzer at the warehouse door sounded. I'd had that installed recently. Made deliveries and visitors easier. "If you'll excuse me, I should go answer that." I gestured toward the loveseat in my office. "Please make yourself comfortable."

I hurried to answer the door. It was the breakfast pastries I'd ordered from Mummy's. They'd only just started a delivery service and I wasn't about to let them stop on account of lack of business. I tipped the delivery guy and took the shopping bag from him, pulling out the boxes as I walked back. Both held the same delicious breakfast goodies: cinnamon rolls, blueberry muffins, lemon poppy seed scones, and cheese danishes.

I left one box on the employee break room table, ditched the bag in the trash, sent Juni a quick text about the goodies, then took the other box back to my office. Sanders took up so much of the loveseat that I was surprised Olive had managed to find an inch for herself, but she didn't seem to mind being squished. I set the box on the coffee table and pulled back the lid. "A little something while we wait."

"Mmm." Sanders smiled blissfully. "Those look

wonderful."

"They're from a great little diner down the street, Mummy's. Can I get you some coffee?"

"No, I'm fine." He went for one of the cinnamon rolls, which is what I would have started with too. Those things were massive and gooey and intensely delicious.

I glanced at Olive. "Would you like some coffee?"

She extricated herself from the loveseat and stood. "I can get my own. Where is it?"

"Employee break room next door, but I don't mind, really."

She waved her hand as she tucked her notebook into her messenger bag. "You don't need to wait on me."

"Okay, if you say so. I'll just call the car service."

"Great, thank you." She left and I dialed. Sanders was busy with the pastries.

A man answered the service's phone. "Executive Limos, where can we drive you today?"

"Hi, this is Jayne Frost. I have a car coming to my shop in Nocturne Falls today and I was wondering if I could get it sooner than it's scheduled."

"Let me check." He hummed softly for a few seconds. "Looks like the car is already on its way. I'll let the driver know to check in as soon as he gets there. That should give you an extra ten minutes."

"Thank you so much."

"Have a good day."

I hung up as Olive returned, a to-go cup of coffee in hand. I nodded at her. "The car will be here a few minutes early."

"Excellent. Is everything else on the schedule good?"

I picked up the paper off my desk. "Yes. We're at the library until eleven, then we have lunch at Howler's." I'd been told Sanders loved cheeseburgers and that was the best place I knew to get one. "After that, it's back here for some down time before the signing at three. That ends at six, and we're due at the Ellingham estate at eight for a welcome reception and cocktail party in Tempus' honor."

I looked at Sanders. He'd moved on to the cheese danishes and his mouth was too full to speak. I glanced at Olive. "Sound good?"

She'd been ticking things off on her notepad. "Sounds perfect."

My phone buzzed. I checked the screen. The car service was here.

Let the games begin.

"Is that a funeral home?" Olive asked as we pulled into the library parking lot.

"Not anymore, but it was." I looked at the building next door. I'd asked the librarian about it myself when I'd come to set things up, but Birdie Caruthers, the sheriff's aunt, had known more. "It's sort of in limbo right now. The building isn't being used for anything. Long story, but there's basically a dispute over the ownership."

"Oh," she said, still staring at it. A shiver ran through her and she laughed. "Sorry, but it's a little creepy."

I'd thought the same thing too when I'd first seen it. "Agreed, but I promise there are no bodies in there."

Sanders clucked his tongue. "Sleep and death are closely related, you know."

Actually, I hadn't. I smiled brightly. "Is that so?"

Thankfully, getting out of the car put an end to that conversation. Once we were inside, the focus became the event.

And it went well. Great, actually. The first kid fell asleep before Sanders finished page one. After that, the event went by in a blur thanks to all the interested parents wanting to know if they could reserve a book at the signing. I had a hundred on hand in the warehouse, but I could get more. And I'd need to now, since the forty parents in attendance had each spoken for at least one. Some two.

Fortunately, Olive was on top of it. She handed me a list. "We've got requests for fifty-three books altogether."

"Wow. That's amazing." I added calling my dad to my mental to-do list for when we got back. He could have shipping put a few additional boxes in our Santa's Bag and we'd be in good shape. He'd probably need to get more printed, but that was for him to worry about. Right now, I was minutes away from figuring out how to mow down a burger while still making small talk and looking ladylike. At least I hoped I was minutes away from lunch. My stomach was rumbling. "Do you think Sanders is ready to go eat?"

She looked in his direction. He was surrounded by kids and parents and practically glowing with happiness. "Probably. I'll have to pull him away, or they'll talk to him forever."

"He looks so happy, though." I didn't want to be the one to crash his party.

She tapped a finger on her notepad. "We're on a schedule."

I tried not to react. Sanders was paying her to do

her job and I wasn't about to tell her to do it different-ly. "We are, that's true."

She trotted off to his side, where she tugged on his sleeve until he bent to listen to her. She said some-thing briefly, then he straightened and said his goodbyes.

I didn't know what Olive had said to him, but Sanders had shifted gears as smoothly as my uncle's sleigh. The woman was impressive. He hadn't seemed upset to leave, either.

We walked into Howler's fifteen minutes later. Bridget greeted us at the hostess stand. "Welcome to Howler's. I'm Bridget, the owner, and I'm so pleased you could join us today."

Sanders smiled and shook her hand. "I've been told you make a mean burger."

"We do," Bridget said. "And we'll fix it any way you like."

"Excellent," Sanders said. "I'll have three to start with."

The man's appetite was impressive, but I think I mentioned that.

Bridget grinned. "Let me get you to your booth then. I've reserved the big one in the back so you'll have lots of room and privacy. Right this way."

We followed her like a row of ducklings following their mother. Olive, then Sanders, then me. Bridget brought us to the booth, which was the last one on the right-hand side and sort of tucked away by itself. She stepped out of the way, her armful of menus clutched to her chest, so we could sit.

Olive slid in first, her gaze expectantly on Sanders.

He took the opposite bench, filling that side of the generous booth to capacity. I sat next to Olive, although 'next to' wasn't exactly correct. We could have fit two more people between us.

Bridget handed out the menus, opening Sanders' to the burger section. Olive buried her face in hers. I think she'd been expecting to sit next to Sanders. Probably so she could go over that blasted schedule again. But really, there wasn't room for her over there.

Bridget took our drink orders and left us to peruse the offerings.

I looked at my menu out of habit, but I knew what I wanted. The steak sandwich with sweet potato fries and a side of mac-n-cheese. I had a feeling tonight's shindig at Elenora's was going to be all about dollhouse-sized bites of food served on miniature spoons. I needed to fortify myself.

I set my menu down and was about to fill Sanders and Olive in on my suspicions when a familiar voice said my name.

"Jayne? You have a minute?"

I looked up and straight into Cooper Sullivan's gorgeous sky-blue eyes. "Sure, what's up?"

"I need a moment. Privately." He smiled oddly and nodded to my lunch companions. "Sorry to interrupt, I just need to borrow Jayne for a second. I'll have her back as quickly as possible."

"No problem," Sanders said.

I got out of my seat. Cooper took my hand and led me to a spot by the doors to the kitchen. "What's up? You look spooked."

He shook his head. "I am. I had the worst dream

last night." His hand tightened on mine and his voice lowered. "I dreamed you were trapped in a burning house." His Adam's apple jumped. "And I couldn't get to you in time."

"Coop, I'm fine." But he was clearly upset by this.

"I see that. But I've had this sense of dread hanging over me all day. I just had to see you. Had to touch you." He stared at my hand. "Had to know you were okay."

"Feel better now?"

He smiled. "I do. You look great, by the way. Not that you don't always look great but this isn't a look I see you in all the time." He gave me the once-over. "Sort of Corporate Jayne. I dig it."

"Thanks. Wanted to look professional with Tempus here and all. Which reminds me, I should get back."

"I know. You've got a job to do. See you tonight, beautiful."

I smiled back. "See you tonight, Coop."

He winked and took off.

I watched him longer than I should have. The man was so handsome it made my sugar teeth ache. I couldn't wait to see him in a tux. Or Greyson, for that matter, although there was no guarantee that's what the vampire would have on—with him, you never knew. But with Cooper? Oh, he was the classic, all-American elf. He'd be in a tux and he'd look so good that swooning would come back into fashion.

I joined Tempus and Olive just as our server arrived with our drinks. "Sorry about the interruption."

"You don't have to worry about me, Jayne," Tem-

31

pus answered. "I don't need to be entertained every moment of the day."

"I appreciate that." He was easygoing, I'd give him that. Which sort of made me wonder why Olive was always on the verge of a nervous twitch. Was Tempus difficult in private? I didn't want to speculate. It could just be that's who Olive was.

We ordered and then, to make Olive happy, ran through the schedule one more time. I watched Tempus for any signs of irritation or short temper, but found none. I decided Olive was just twitchy.

Lunch arrived and we ate, Sanders adding two more burgers to his order as soon as he tasted the first one. Bridget was happy to accommodate him, getting them out in record time, but it kept us at the restaurant longer than scheduled.

Lingering meant I gave in and had a piece of peach cobbler. Delicious, but one mouthful too many, after my large lunch. I almost had to roll myself back to the warehouse. Thankfully, it was close.

My guests might be able to take a little catnap before the big signing this afternoon, but I had work to do. I said goodbye to Olive and Sanders at the elevator, then went into my office to call my dad.

I shook the globe, then set it down while I grabbed a Dr Pepper from the employee breakroom fridge. I was stuffed, but I needed the caffeine or I was going to be face-down and snoring. My father appeared as I sat at my desk. "Hey Dad."

"Hi, Jayne. How's it going?"

"Great." I twisted the top off the soda and took a swig. I might need a steady supply of these to get me through the rest of this day—and night. "So great I already need more books. The reading at the library went so well that the parents there reserved more than half my stock."

"I can get you another hundred. Think that will do it or do you want more?"

"Can I get two hundred? Just to be sure."

"Absolutely." He beamed. "This book is going to be a hit, huh?"

"It sure looks that way." I tipped the bottle at him. "Especially if word spreads. Which I think it will."

My dad nodded. "That's great news. You're doing a wonderful job."

His words were kind, but more flattery than anything. I shrugged. "I'm sure the book would have been a success no matter which store you launched it from."

"Perhaps." His dark blue brows wiggled. "But we had to have someone in charge who could not only launch the book, but take good care of Sanders. And who better than North Pole royalty?"

"Yeah, but you guys made it sound like he was going to be difficult. So far he's been easy as pie. And his assistant really is the one taking care of him."

My father's expression shifted and he shook his head. "*So far* being the operative words. He can be difficult, Jayne. Demanding. Impatient. Occasionally quick-tempered."

Something dawned on me. I straightened. "You sent him here because you and Uncle Kris thought Sanders was less likely to play the prima donna card with me, didn't you? Because I'm the Winter Princess.

33

After all, we're practically family."

I already knew the answer by looking at my dad's face. He'd been caught. It wasn't a look I'd seen on him often, but it wasn't one I was about to forget, either. "It might have occurred to us as a side benefit."

"Uh-huh." I gave my father a stern glare. "Just get those books here on time or you're going to have another diva on your hands."

"Yes, my darling daughter." He grinned. "Love you."

"Love you, too."

We both hung up and the snow settled.

I sat back, surprised I hadn't caught on to my father's and uncle's craftiness until now. I took another sip of my Dr Pepper. But they were right. Sanders might be treating me differently because of who I was.

We were sort of family. Sort of. Sanders wasn't exactly a typical elf. He was considered an elemental. A creature beyond the definitions of winter or summer. One who could move space or time and harness the kind of magic that most ordinary elves couldn't. Father Time, Mother Nature, the Grim Reaper, Lady Luck—you get the idea. Not all elemental elves are as all-powerful as the big names in that group, but that's a good thing, because there are more of them than you think.

My uncle Kris was one too. So was my mom, but she was one of those elementals whose powers weren't much to speak of. My dad had some elemental in him, too. What can I say? It runs in the royal bloodline.

My uncle, though, he's completely elemental. I

34

know, most people think Santa is a full-blooded winter elf—and he really is in many ways. Second only to my father, he was the elf who most fully embodied the spirit of winter. But the kind of magic my uncle Kris had was beyond what my father had. Kris Kringle could bend time. He showed off that skill every Christmas Eve.

And in case you haven't figured it out, that means I have a little elemental in me, too. Not that it's meant anything so far in my life. Probably won't, either. The more that line gets diluted, the weaker it becomes.

It's not a big deal. I've got plenty of cold magic and I'm perfectly happy with that.

But fully elemental elves, like Sanders (and yes, my uncle at times) could be temperamental. I knew that. I just hadn't expected my dad and uncle to be so sneaky. I should have, though. *I* certainly could be and the icicle doesn't fall far from the eave.

I put my soda down and went to check the Santa's Bag for the shipment of books. The bag really *was* a bag. And every store had one. The big red velvet sacks were about three feet by four feet, but they were bigger on the inside. Way bigger.

The bag was one of the best-known magical creations to come out of the NP, but also the most secret. It was basically a direct portal from the NP to wherever the bag was. They were how the stores got whatever stock they needed, when they needed it. Other stuff could be sent through the bags too (which is how my mom had sent my winter clothes and party dresses), but nothing living.

Because that might get weird.

35

Anyway, when the bag was full, it was filled out like a box, no matter what was inside. When it was empty, it was…well, empty. Flat. Made it easy to see when there was a shipment.

The one in my warehouse was full.

I backtracked into the store to get Kip. I waved at Juniper, who was busy at the register, and kept going. I found him in the vehicles area, showing Rowley a few things. "I need some help in the warehouse, Kip. Extra stock to be taken care of."

"You got it." He looked at the older man. "You okay by yourself?"

Rowley shooed him off. "I'm just fine. I need anything, I'll go see Miss Juniper."

"All right." Kip turned to me. "All yours."

"Thanks. There's a second shipment of books to be added to the signing stock. I want another hundred put on the front table. The rest please stack close to the shop door in the warehouse so they're easy to get to when we need more."

"I'll get it done."

"Thanks. I'm going to check the signing area one more time." I was sure it was fine, but I felt like it needed to be done. Olive was going to either way, so I'd better make sure.

We'd set up the signing in the kids' play area. I wasn't keen to rope that section off, but it was the best spot in the store for a thing like this. The toys normally available for play had been shelved, the beanbag seats cleared, and a beautiful table and chair had been arranged near the back wall. There was a small display of books on the table, but the rest of the books were up front, where Kip would soon be adding more.

Anyone who wanted a signed book had to buy one first. Juniper and Buttercup would be running the register, Holly would be checking receipts in the signing line, Rowley would be mingling on the floor, and Kip would be keeping an eye on stock.

Olive would be tending to Tempus, of course.

And I would be making sure nothing went wrong. Nothing.

Because the last thing I needed was for the Sandman to have a meltdown in front of a store full of people *and* press.

Did I mention that I'd invited the Tombstone? That was the local Nocturne Falls paper. I'd only gotten confirmation yesterday that they were sending a reporter and a photographer. No idea who, but Delaney said if it was Piper Hodge, I'd need to watch myself around her. Her parents own the Tombstone, so that meant she got dibs on whatever stories she liked and if she liked this one, it might not be the article I was hoping for.

Delaney said Piper wasn't always out to show the best side of things.

Let me back up a tick. Delaney and I had been chatting a lot since she'd convinced Elenora that the Sandman's visit was perfect reason to throw a party— secretly, I think Delaney was hoping to get some tips from him on how to get her new baby to sleep more.

Anyway, Piper was apparently an ex-girlfriend of Delaney's husband, Hugh Ellingham, so Delaney filled me in on everything she knew about the woman. And then I reminded Delaney that I was (in a roundabout way) the reason Piper had turned blue a few months back.

We might have bonded a little more over that.

Of course, Piper was human and didn't really know what had caused all the chaos in Nocturne Falls this past August (an imp I had accidentally let out of a box), but there had been enough murmuring in town for word to get around that I might have been involved somehow.

Kind of made calling the Tombstone about the book release seem like a two-edged sword now, but I'd been trying to do the best possible job I could on this launch. I wanted to impress my dad and uncle and I knew my dad read the Tombstone, so I figured if I could get a nice mention in there, that would be a great way to show him how hard I was working.

But snowballs, what if Piper was the reporter the paper sent and she wrote something up about how the book was awful and the store was lousy and...? I took a deep breath.

I was letting my head get the best of me. That wouldn't happen. For one thing, the book was amazing. Sanders was charismatic and instantly likeable in person so if Piper met him, she'd be just as swayed as everyone else. And for another thing, the store was awesome. It was cheery and filled with toys and happiness and Christmas spirit.

Unless she was Scrooge, everything would be fine.

I still needed some sugar. The idea that Piper might come with the hopes of making us (or me) look bad had created an ache in me that could only be eased by something sweet. I looked in the employee breakroom for a chocolate truffle or a cookie. Nothing. It was like a herd of yetis had come through and cleaned us out. Minus the drool and lingering smell of wet socks.

But I'm not a quitter. I knew where to get my fix. I slipped into the store and went behind the register. "I need something."

Juniper was ringing up a customer but answered me without looking, her voice soft. "You know where it is."

"Thanks." I crouched down and reached into one of the cubbies under the counter for a metal cash box. I pulled it out. A handwritten label on a strip of duct tape across the top said *feminine supplies*. The supplies inside were indeed feminine—they were put there by Juni and Buttercup and now Holly—but they weren't *those* kinds of feminine supplies.

I opened the box and took out a Rocket bar and a Scooter patty, then slid the stash back to its spot and stood. I palmed the candy as best I could. "I'll replace these as soon as I can."

"We're chill," Juniper said. "As many snacks and goodies as you've supplied us with in the breakroom, those are on Buttercup and me."

"Thanks." I gave her a little hip bump and went back to my office. I downed the Rocket bar in record time, then took a breather as the sugar kicked in. I was starting to feel better. The time on my phone said one forty-three. I had an hour and seventeen minutes before the signing was underway. Maybe I could catch a quick twenty winks.

I picked up the phone and hit the button for the register while I ate the Scooter patty.

Juni picked up. "You need more?"

"No, no. Just wanted to see if everything's good?" I asked around the chocolatey mouthful of peanuts, caramel, and marshmallow.

"Yep. Same as it was three minutes ago when you were in here. You're kind of spinning yourself up, you know."

"I know. Which is why I was thinking maybe I should go upstairs and lay down for a little bit."

"Do it."

"Will you be my wake-up call? I'll set my alarm, too, but just in case—"

"I'm all over it like white on ice. Two fifteen?"

"Perfect. Thanks."

"Sweet dreams." She hung up.

I threw the candy wrappers away, turned off the light in my office and went upstairs. Spider was sprawled on the couch so I joined him, lying down carefully so my clothes and hair wouldn't end up too mussed. I set my phone to go off in twenty minutes and closed my eyes.

Sleep eluded me at first. My brain was too busy. I took a few deep breaths and petted Spider, who was now curled at my side. I focused on the silkiness of his fur and the way his little body vibrated as he purred.

Finally the tug of sleep pulled me in.

I woke a few minutes later in the same sort of panic I'd felt the night before, except this time I had no memory of what had caused my heart to pound and my nervous system to freak out.

I sat up, my chest heaving, and tried to calm myself. It was easier in the light of day than in a pitch-black room. There were no lurking shadows or strange shapes. I checked the time on my phone.

I'd been asleep twelve minutes.

Son of a nutcracker. I was more wrecked now than before I laid down. I huffed out a breath and swung my feet onto the floor. Nothing to do but get on with it.

"What's wrong, Mama?" Spider butted his head against my side.

I scratched it. "I'm a little stressed. But I'll be fine."

He sat next to me. "What's stressed?"

"Something cats know nothing about." I patted his head, slipped my shoes back on, and got up. "I have to go back downstairs now, but I'll feed you first." One of us might as well be happy.

41

I gave him a can of Chicken Party, then grabbed another Dr Pepper and went to my office. I checked my reflection in the little mirror I kept in my desk drawer. The hairspray I'd shellacked my head with this morning seemed to be holding, so at least I had that going for me.

I drank about half the Dr Pepper, said a little prayer I wouldn't burp in Sanders face, and ran one final check of everything in the store.

Juniper and Kip were on top of things, and Rowley, who was working the overlap shift, was already on the floor. The store was just as perfect as I'd left it. And people were already in the shop, buying the book and getting in line for the signing.

All we needed now was Sanders. I stood by the register and thought about waiting in the warehouse, but that might be weird—just standing there, twiddling my thumbs. I could go back to my office, but then I'd have to make sure I listened for the elevator. Maybe I should just stay here and greet him when he walked in.

But what if he needed something ahead of time? I suppose that's what Olive was for, but—

"Hey."

I looked over at Juniper. "What?"

"You're biting your lip and your forehead is all scrunched up. It's going to be fine."

"I know." I smiled weakly. Then made myself straighten up and repeated my words with more conviction. "I know. And you're right."

A thin blond woman walked in, cutting straight through the gathering crowd, and came up to me.

42

"You must be Jayne Frost."

She had one of those voices that sounded like she was speaking with her back teeth clenched. Very upper-crusty. "I am. What can I help you with?"

She smiled, revealing even white teeth that went perfectly with her slim, tan ankle pants, lavender sweater set, and pearls. She stuck her hand out. "I'm Piper Hodge. From the Tombstone. I'm here to do a piece about the book signing."

I shook her hand, willing myself not to react with anything but the royal grace I'd had drilled into me as a child. I smiled back. "It's a pleasure to meet you. We love the Tombstone. And we're so glad to have you with us today for this special event."

"This is a lovely store you have here. The whole Christmas thing is so well done."

"Thank you." I relaxed. Didn't seem like she was out for blood after all. "Would you like to see the signing area before we get underway?"

"That would be lovely." She gestured behind her at the man who'd come in with her. "This is my photographer, Joe Simmons. He'll be doing all the shots today."

Joe waved. I waved back. This was going to be okay.

I showed Piper around, answered a few questions and then, at five minutes to three, excused myself to get Sanders. He had to be in the warehouse by now.

The elevator door opened a few seconds after I exited the shop. I stood there, smiling at my perfect timing. I nodded to Sanders and Olive as they walked out. "Have a nice rest?"

He nodded. He'd changed into a new set of fancy pajamas that were deep marine blue. Very calming. His hourglass was on the cord at his waist, gleaming brightly. "I always sleep well."

I laughed. "I imagine you do. Ready to sign?"

"Absolutely. I can't wait."

"Good." I glanced at Olive. Her messenger bag was slung across her body and bulging with supplies. What kind of supplies, I wasn't sure, but Sanders wasn't going to want for a thing. Still, I had to check. "Is there anything you need from me?"

She looked at her notepad before answering, then patted her bag. "I have a supply of the gel pens we've chosen for the signing, hand sanitizer, several bottles of water, three kinds of mints, a box of chocolates, two sandwiches, a thermos of soup, and a roll of *Signed by the Author* stickers." She hesitated. "There's a pack of tissues in there too."

My eyes widened. "Wow. You're really ready. We could get shipwrecked and be okay."

Sanders laughed. Olive didn't. I felt the need to fix that, since I really had meant it as a compliment. "We should all be so lucky to have someone like you in our lives. I wish I was half as organized and prepared."

She didn't quite smile, but something about her lightened.

The door from the shop opened and Juniper stuck her head through. "We're lined up and ready to go in here. And it's packed. Kip's going to be restocking before you know it."

"Awesome." I gave her a thumbs up. "We're on our way."

She closed the door and I looked at Sanders. "Let's do this."

And we did. Sanders worked the crowd like the charmer he was. They were mesmerized by him. Kip stayed busy filling the front table with books, and by the top of the second hour I was on the globe to my dad again, getting another hundred books sent through.

The store was organized madness in the most glorious way. People were happy and chatting and *shopping*. Buttercup and Juniper kept the lines moving, and the register never stopped cha-chinging. Piper talked with people in line and Joe snapped pics of the crowds inside and out. Holly and Olive handled the customers waiting for autographs like they'd been doing it for years.

And every time I checked on Sanders, he was smiling and laughing along with everyone around him. He posed for pictures and selfies, and the mood in the store was more than just festive. It had become a party.

We were a blizzard of activity. I wasn't still more than thirty seconds. No one was. The adrenalin rush of it all had me high. This was beyond sugar. It was almost magical. And to think I'd been worried there wasn't enough caffeine in my system.

The time flew by and when the signing came to an end, there were two books in the display window, another five on the table by the door and one more Buttercup had stuck under the counter because of a torn page. I did a quick tally in my head. We'd sold four hundred ninety-two books.

I almost fell over.

I couldn't wait to tell my dad and uncle. But I would have to. First, I needed to usher Sanders out of the store. The signing was over, but just like at the library, he was mobbed with people. I sidled up to Olive. "The cocktail party starts at eight thirty, but the car will be here at eight. Elenora wanted a few moments with Sanders all to herself."

She nodded. "That gives us about an hour to get ready. I'll get him moving now or we'll never make it in time." Her eyes narrowed like she was thinking. "And he'll need to talk about this, get it out of his system."

"Well, there will be plenty of people willing to listen at the party. It *is* in his honor."

"True." Olive nodded. "Good job setting that up."

"I can't take the credit. My friend Delaney was responsible. Her and her grandmother-in-law. It's at her house, after all."

"Elenora."

"That's the one."

Olive looked pensive. "I've never met a vampire before."

"You have nothing to worry about." I smiled. "I promise."

"I believe you." She tapped her watch. "All right, time to get the king moving."

I'd never heard her call him that before. I clasped my hands in front of me and gave my team a nod to let them know we were wrapping things up. With that prompt, they started herding people back to the main area of the store.

Olive had Sanders out of the shop in less than ten minutes. On their way to the warehouse door, she glanced my way. "We'll see you at the car."

"Very good." That was my cue to get moving too. With Sanders gone, the excitement was returning to normal levels. Buttercup and Holly would handle the remaining hours of business, and Rowley would stay on another hour to work on setting up the signing area for tomorrow and restocking everywhere else. The store had gotten a bit disheveled with all the customers milling about, but thankfully books weren't the only things they'd bought.

I walked with Juniper and Kip to the elevator. "What a day, huh?"

"I'll say." Juniper wiggled her fingers. "The last time we were that busy was Christmas Eve."

Kip nodded. "And that will be here before you know it."

I smiled. "Let's get through tomorrow before we think about that. One more signing, then we can start prepping for Christmas madness."

The elevator doors opened and we all got on.

Juniper pushed the buttons for two and three. "I can't believe we have to do that all over again tomorrow."

"I know." I leaned back for a moment. "I can't decide if we'll be busier because of word of mouth or dead because everyone who wanted a book already got one. Regardless, we have to be prepared to get slammed again."

The elevator stopped on the second floor and Juniper and I got out. "Have a good night, Kip. Be ready to keep us stocked up again tomorrow."

"I will be. Enjoy your party."

"Thanks." I waved as the doors shut.

"Speaking of the party," Juniper said, "you need help getting ready?"

We walked toward our apartments. "I wouldn't mind the company."

She grinned. "Cool. Lemme go put my comfy clothes on and I'll be right over."

"I'll leave it unlocked." I went in and was immediately rushed by Spider.

"Hungry! So hungry!" He wove through my legs. "Hungry hungry—"

"I get it, you're hungry." I scooped him up and kissed his velvet nose. "Let's go feed you before someone calls animal control and reports me as a bad cat mother."

Purring, he butted his head against my chin. "Spider love Mama."

"And Mama loves Spider." I set him back on the floor, put his dirty dish in the sink and filled a clean one with the required can of Chicken Party.

Juniper came in wearing sweats and a Hello Kitty T-shirt. "Okay, what's first?"

"Me. In the shower. Then I need to fix my make-up, put my dress on, do my hair, and add the accessories." My stomach rumbled. "Um, actually, would you mind making me a PB&J? I thought I'd be okay after my big lunch, but I must have burned it all off running around the shop."

"Sure thing." She picked up one of Spider's favorite toys, a fishing pole with a feather lure at the end.

"Then I'll wear your cat out while you shower."

I glanced at him wolfing down his food. "Maybe wait on that. I don't want to clean up puke in an evening gown."

Her brows lifted and she put the toy down. "Good call. I'll stick to just making the sandwich."

I headed for the shower. "I won't be long. Help yourself to whatever." When I popped out of the shower a few minutes later, I could hear the TV, and Juni talking to Spider. He was not, however, talking back. I wondered if he'd ever start talking in front of other people.

I added more eyeliner and shadow and another coat of mascara, then freshened my blush and set everything with powder. Lipstick could wait until the dress was on. I went to my bedroom and into the walk-in closet.

My mom had sent a selection of my formalwear, but there was only one dress I was really interested in: my gown from last year's Yule Ball. The shape and color were simple. Narrow straps gave way to a body-hugging column of black stretch jersey. But this was magical fae fabric, a gift from my parents. It had been woven to reproduce the aurora borealis with every movement.

I slipped the dress on and turned in front of the mirror. Shimmers of green and blue iridescence shot down from my hip. I turned again and a wave of magenta danced across the bodice. No one else would have a dress like this, which was great, but what I really loved about it was that it had been a gift from my parents.

I retrieved the jewelry case my mother had sent along with the dresses and went back to the bathroom to fix my hair.

"You need help yet?" Juni called out.

"Not yet."

"Okay. Your sandwich is ready."

"Be out in a sec."

The updo was easy, something my mom had taught me as soon as I was old enough to attend royal functions. A high ponytail, a couple of twists, a few pins and done. The perfect backdrop for the rest of what I'd be wearing this evening.

Satisfied, I added a slick of gloss instead of lipstick, then took the jewelry case and walked into the living room. "What do you think?"

Juniper gasped. "Oh, Jayne. That dress."

I smiled and did a twirl. "It was a gift from my parents. Isn't it something? I love it."

She turned the TV off and stood. "I can see why. Is that fae fabric?"

"Yep."

She sighed. "Totally fit for a princess. Your parents are awesome." Then she put her hands on her hips. "And you didn't need my help getting ready at all."

I held out the jewelry box. "You can help me with this." I opened it to reveal my diamond tiara, the Winter Princess crown.

"Get out." She grinned. "Can I try it on? No, never mind, that was wrong of me to ask."

I laughed. "You can try it on tomorrow before I send it back. For now, help me get the combs into my hair so it doesn't shift during the night."

I sat in one of the kitchen chairs and ate the PB&J while she wiggled it into place. "Is that okay?"

I swallowed. "Really get it on there." She gave it

another push and I felt the combs dig into my scalp. "Perfect."

She gazed into the jewelry box. "Are you wearing anything else out of here?"

"That crystal necklace and those diamond hoops."

She picked up the necklace, brought it over my head and fastened the clasp. "There you go. Beautiful."

"Thanks for the help. And the sandwich. That should hold me until I can eat some tiny hors d'oeuvres." I put the hoops on and stood. "All I need are shoes and my bag and I'm good to go." I looked at the clock on the microwave. "With twelve minutes to spare."

"Which means Cooper is probably downstairs already."

"Or will be in two minutes." I gathered up my things—my keys, my lipgloss, my phone, some cash, and a bandaid in case my shoes give me a blister—and tucked them into my little velvet evening purse. Then I went to my closet and slipped on my shoes, medium-high strappy black heels that I hoped wouldn't be too much to spend a long night in.

I walked back out.

"You look so good." Juniper was waiting at the door. "You mind if I walk down with you? I want to see Cooper in his tux."

"Sure. You can take a picture of us."

"Great. Are you sending one to your parents?"

"Maybe." But probably not. I still hadn't told them Cooper was in Nocturne Falls. I would, but not tonight.

I locked up and we went down in the elevator. Cooper was standing in the warehouse, waiting, so he must have come through the shop door.

He let out a long, low whistle as Juniper and I got off. His eyes lit up and he grinned like he'd just won something. "Princess Jayne."

As the elevator doors closed behind us, I cocked one hip out, trying not to melt at the sight of him in his tuxedo. It fit him as perfectly as I'd known it would. I remembered to breathe. Looking that good ought to be illegal. "Yes, Fireman Cooper?"

His grin widened and Juniper laughed softly behind me. He let out a long sigh. "You look absolutely amazing."

He closed the gap between us and took my hand, lifting it to his mouth and kissing my knuckles. "Even if I have to share this night, I'm happy to be at your side for part of the evening. But I'm really glad I get you first."

Juniper snorted. "You look great, Coop. And now I'm going back upstairs."

I turned. "Wait a sec. You were going to take our picture."

"Oh, yep. Forgot. Sorry."

I fished my phone out, brought up the camera, and handed it over.

Juni snapped a few as Cooper and I posed, then gave it back. "You guys have a great evening. You both look fantastic."

"Thanks," Cooper and I both said.

She was about to hit the button to call the elevator when the doors opened and Tempus and Olive stepped out. She stood to the side to let them pass, then slipped in, waved and was gone.

Tempus and Olive were both in black, Tempus in his fancy pajamas and slippers—this time trimmed in gold—and Olive in a classic sheath dress with a strand of pearls and diamond studs. No heels for her, though. Patent leather flats. A smart choice, I thought, considering how much running she might have to do for Sanders at this event.

"You both look very nice." The usual cord holding Sanders' hourglass had been swapped out for a thick gold chain.

"As do you, Princess." He gave me a little nod. "Very regal. And nice to see some of the crown jewels out this evening."

I touched my tiara. "I don't wear it often, but this seemed like the perfect occasion."

"Indeed."

I put my hand on Cooper's arm. "This is Cooper Sullivan, summer elf and Nocturne Falls fireman. He's my date for the first half of the evening."

Sanders stuck his hand out. "Tempus Sanders. Pleasure to meet you, son."

"Likewise." Cooper shook his hand, then looked at Olive, whom Sanders and I had failed to introduce.

I hurried to rectify that. "And this is Olive Pine, Mr. Sanders' right-hand woman."

Cooper, being Cooper, took her extended hand, lifted it to his mouth and kissed her knuckles just as he had mine. "It's a pleasure to meet the woman in charge. You look lovely this evening, but then I imagine you always do."

Olive smiled—and maybe even blushed a little. "Thank you, Mr. Sullivan."

"Please," he said. "Call me Cooper. Or Coop."

"Okay, Cooper. And please call me Olive."

"They're going to call us late to arrive," Tempus grumped.

"Yes," I said. "We should go. I'm sure the car is waiting."

We headed out to the limo and piled in (as gracefully as people in formal clothes can pile), and twenty minutes later we were walking through Elenora Ellingham's front doors.

Her house was half the size of the winter palace, but about equally as grand. I felt at ease because of that. And also a little homesick.

Elenora greeted us at the door. She was a handsome older woman, but she had the shape of someone much younger. I guessed that was because she was a vampire. Or good genes. But the vampire thing had to help. Either way, she was dressed modestly in a lavender-colored silk gown with tasteful beading. Her jewels were not quite so simple, however. At her ears, throat, wrists, and fingers, diamonds and amethysts sparkled in abundance.

I'd thought my mother's suggestion that I wear my tiara a little overkill. Now I was glad I had it.

Elenora dropped into a delicate curtsey as I approached. "Princess. So good of you to come."

I hadn't expected that. "Thank you for opening your home…" I wasn't sure what to call her.

She straightened and smiled, her fangs not visible although I knew they were there. "Please, call me

Elenora."

"Then please call me Jayne." I stepped to the side and introduced my party. "Elenora, this is your guest of honor, Tempus Sanders, the Sandman himself."

Her smile grew a little and she clasped his hand between both of hers. "What a pleasure to meet you, Tempus. May I call you Tempus?"

"Of course," he replied. "What a lovely home you have."

"So kind of you. Let me give you the tour."

And just like that, they were off on their own, leaving Cooper, Olive and me in the foyer. One of the staff, a man in a butler's uniform, stepped forward and stretched out his hand toward the open double doors a few yards behind him. "The ballroom is right this way."

I glanced at Olive and Cooper. "Well, I don't know about you two, but I'm going in to get a drink."

"I don't drink when I'm working," Olive said.

Cooper looked at her. "Nobody's working tonight." He stuck his elbow out, offering her his arm. "Come on, we'll go get one together."

She stared at him, hesitating, then finally looped her arm through his. "Just one."

"Just one." He winked at me. "See you in there, Jay." Then he and Olive strode off toward the ballroom.

I could have kissed him for being so sweet to Olive. And I would, later. I followed them into the space Elenora had set aside for tonight's gathering.

The room was enormous, as a ballroom should be. The space was decked out in tranquil colors—dusky purple, gentle roses and deep blues. The colors of twilight. Fairy lights twinkled among the flower arrangements and off to one side, a woman in a black evening gown played a baby grand piano. The music and the decorations were all very soothing. Perfect for a party honoring the King of Dreams.

I just hoped I could keep my eyes open.

Cooper and Olive were at one of the three bars. He waved me over. "What would you like, Jay?"

I smiled at him. "You know what I like."

He nodded and turned to the bartender. "Do you have moscato?"

The bartender lifted a bottle and started to pour. Elenora had done well. She either stocked every possible thing her guests might want, or she'd found out that winter elves liked sweet things. That made me wonder what the food situation was going to be like.

"Jayne!"

I turned at the sound of my name and saw Delaney walking in.

I waved, happy to see a friendly face. We met in the middle of the floor. "Hi there. How are you? How is George?"

"We're both great. This is the first time I've been out of the house since he was born. I sort of miss him already, but I can manage a few hours." Then she put her hands to her mouth. "Oh, you look so good. I don't know what I like more, the dress or the tiara. I want a tiara! I wish I was a princess."

I laughed as her husband joined us. "I'm surprised you don't already have one. You don't have to be a princess to wear one, you know."

"Hugh." She nudged him. "Did you hear that? Jayne says I could wear a tiara too."

He put his arm around her. "Well, you are *my* princess."

I couldn't help but smile at his comment. "You two are so perfect together."

Delaney leaned into Hugh. "We are, aren't we? But wait until you see Sebastian and Tessa together."

Hugh added. "My brother is besotted. It's rather a nice change after all his years of being the family curmudgeon."

"I'd love to meet them." I looked around. People were trickling in but there was no sign of Elenora and Sanders returning yet. Or snacks. Blast my perpetually empty stomach.

"Why don't I go to the bar and get us some drinks?" Hugh said. "Delaney, what would you like?"

She held onto his arm. "I'm fine. But get Jayne something."

"I'm good too. Cooper's getting my drink." I looked toward the bar. "Actually, he and Olive are on their way over. What I'd really like are some truffles. You didn't happen to bring any did you?"

"As a matter of fact..." Delaney pointed over my shoulder. "My shop supplied some of the goodies being served tonight."

I turned to see what she'd pointed at. A slew of uniformed servers glided out from some room beyond the ballroom, their silver trays filled with sweets of every description. My heart fluttered with happiness.

"Delaney, I might be a princess, but you're the

Queen of Sugar. That is exactly what I need to get through this night."

She beamed. "I told Elenora winter elves like their sugar. The Sandman is a winter elf, isn't he?"

"Pretty much." Wasn't my place to explain the whole elemental thing.

Cooper and Olive joined us and I introduced her to Delaney and Hugh. By that time, the ballroom was starting to fill up and I still hadn't seen Elenora or Sanders.

I only worried for about thirty seconds more. That's when they strode through the ballroom doors together and Elenora started taking him around the room and introducing him to everyone.

I took a sip of my wine, then nudged Olive, whose eyes were locked onto Sanders. "Must be nice to have a night off, huh?"

She shook her head without taking her gaze off him. "He'll need me for something, you'll see. He always does."

I checked the glass in her hand. I didn't think she'd had a single sip. "Try to enjoy some of the evening, if you can. You've earned a little fun."

She nodded, her eyes straight ahead.

Cooper slipped his arm around my waist and whispered in my ear. "How about a dance, beautiful?"

The piano player had been joined by a bass guitarist and a drummer and the music had gone from easy listening to peppier jazz.

I smiled at him, took another drink, then set my glass on the tray of a passing server. Olive might not be willing to let down her hair, but I was. Metaphorically anyway. "Let's go."

We made our way onto the dance floor, where quite a few other couples were getting their groove on. I rested my left palm on his shoulder as he took my right hand, and off we went.

It was impossible not to smile. "I think the last time we danced was—"

"Homecoming," he finished.

The memory was bittersweet. We'd broken up not long after that, because of the lies of my best friend, Lark. She'd texted both of us a few months back, but Cooper had handled it (not sure how; I didn't ask) and I really hoped that was that. But I didn't want to think about her. "That was a fun night."

"It was. But I like this better."

"Why's that?"

"Because we're adults now."

"You think that would have made a difference?"

His brows pulled together. "Yes. I was too easily swayed by the things Lark told me. I should have talked to you. We might have worked things out."

I nodded. Talking about what-ifs like this always made me a little melancholy. "I should have talked to you, too."

"Instead, we both trusted her."

And I'd had my heart broken. I forced a smile to cover the twang of pain. "But we're here now."

He smiled too, but it looked as forced as mine felt. "Only temporarily, though. In another hour or so, the vampire will be here."

I narrowed my eyes a bit and pursed my lips. "Coop. You're getting a little mopey for no reason. It's not like you're never going to see me again after tonight. We can go out any time you like."

He laughed. "True. How about every night this week then?"

I was about to answer when the music ended and Elenora called out, "Ladies and gentlemen, if I please may have your attention for a moment."

We all turned to look at her. She stood a few steps up on the grand stairway that led to the second-floor balcony.

She lifted her glass. "Please join me in toasting our marvelous guest, Tempus Sanders." She shifted her gaze to him and everyone in the crowd followed. "Thank you for gracing us with your presence this evening, Tempus. I think I speak for us all when I say we will sleep a little better tonight just knowing you're in town."

Everyone laughed appropriately and drank to Tempus.

Elenora waved at the musicians. "On with the party."

The tunes started up again, but Cooper nodded toward someone in the crowd. "The chief is here. I should go say hi. Come on, he likes you."

"He barely knows me."

Cooper snorted. "Maybe that's why he likes you."

I poked him in the arm. "Now you're definitely taking me to dinner. Somewhere nice too. Not Howler's. Which is nice. But you know what I mean."

He took my hand. "Guillermo's it is then."

I let him lead me forward. "Ooo... Italian?"

"Yes. Don't wear white."

"Why?"

He smirked. "Red sauce and all that."

I rolled my eyes at him. "You have so little faith in my eating abilities."

We stopped in front of Titus and Hank Merrow, the fire chief and sheriff, respectively.

Cooper greeted them. "Evening, Chief. Sheriff. You know my date, Jayne Frost."

Both men nodded, but only the chief smiled. Which was standard. "Miss Frost." The chief added, "Nice to see you again."

"Why don't I go get us another round?" Cooper offered. "Chief? Sheriff?"

Both men nodded, lifted the bottles in their hands (something I was shocked Elenora had allowed at her party) and said, "Beer."

Cooper kissed me on the cheek. "Be right back."

Bridget, their sister, popped up next to us as Cooper was leaving. "Hey, gang. Fun night, huh? Anyone seen PJ?"

Hank groaned. "You brought her?"

Bridget shot him a look. "What was I supposed to do, leave her home?"

He shook his head. "You should have gotten Aunt Birdie to take her out."

"Aunt Birdie had bingo."

Hank and Titus nodded, like that was explanation enough. Apparently Birdie's bingo was not to be messed with.

Titus started scanning the crowd. "She's got to be here somewhere."

I leaned toward Bridget. "Who's PJ?"

"Our cousin, Penny Jo. She's visiting for a couple weeks." Bridget shrugged. "I had no choice but to bring her. Besides she's thinking about moving here, so why not?"

"Because," Titus started, "she's a handful. And bound to cause trouble."

Bridget frowned. "She's just...friendly. She's a country girl. That's all."

"Friendly." Hank snorted. "I lock people up for being that kind of friendly."

"Oh, Hank," Bridget sighed. "Leave the kid alone. You know what it's like to be a young werewolf with all those hormones coursing through you. She's sowing some oats. That's all. We all did it."

"Not all of us." He tipped his bottle toward something behind me. "PJ sighting, twelve o'clock. And looks like she's found herself a fireman."

I turned to see what the sheriff was talking about. My mouth fell open and, for the moment, I was powerless to close it.

Son of a nutcracker.

Penny Jo and Cooper stood a few feet away. Cooper's hands were full of drinks, but PJ's hands were full of Cooper.

My stomach tightened. Jealousy? Anger? Annoyance? I wasn't sure. And since Cooper and I weren't exclusive, it didn't matter. I might feel those things, but I couldn't act on them too much. Not without causing some kind of decision to be made, something I wasn't ready to do.

But standing there, not reacting, was tough.

PJ looked like she'd cannonballed into the Dolly Parton end of the gene pool. Twice. She had a mass of blond curls, an hourglass figure that was testing the limits of the blue dress she'd been poured into and a giggly, bouncy personality I could sense from here. Her hands were wrapped around Cooper's arm like someone had told her hanging onto him would make all her dreams come true. And she appeared to be cooing at him.

Cooing.

I'd never wanted to punch a stranger quite so much.

I turned away and took a breath, wishing I had that drink. *Princesses don't punch people in public. Princesses don't punch people in public. Princesses don't—*

"You okay?" Bridget asked. "You look a little green."

Hank grunted before I could answer. "How'd you feel if a woman like that was draped all over Sam?"

"I'd raise hell. Sam and I are exclusive. Jayne and Cooper aren't. But I see your point." Then Bridget elbowed me. "You could always go over there and do something about it."

I gave her a look. "Instigator. But now I know whose team you're on."

She grinned. "What did you expect? Coop's a fireman."

Titus sighed. "I'll go rescue him."

"No, I've got this." Penny Jo might be a werewolf, but I was the Winter Princess. I lifted my chin, called up my social graces and walked over. "Help you with the drinks, Coop?"

"Thanks." He handed me mine and one of the beers. "This is Penny Jo Lamont. She's the Merrows' cousin."

She teetered next to him on her sky-high heels, barely coming up to the notch on his lapel.

I smiled at her. You have no idea how hard that

was. So. Hard. "How nice to meet you, Penny Jo."

Cooper tried to lift his arm free, but PJ seemed more anaconda than werewolf. "Penny Jo, this is Princess Jayne Frost."

That got Penny Jo's attention. She looked at me, her big brown eyes wide. "Princess?" Her gaze went to my tiara. "For real?"

I nodded. "Yes."

Then she put her hand to her chest, which only covered one tiny part of it. "I'm a princess too."

I frowned. "You are?"

"Mmm-hmm. Miss Southern Georgia Peach two years in a row and Sparkle Queen last year. That's an independent pageant." She snorted. "How about that, I'm actually a queen." She wiggled her fingers at me. "I outrank you."

The edges of my vision were starting to go dim.

"Uh, Penny Jo?" Cooper looked at her. "Jayne is a *real* princess. As in actual royalty. She's the Winter Princess. Next in line for the Winter Throne. Currently occupied by her father, Jack Frost." He leaned down a little. "She's also my date."

Had I kissed Cooper yet? Because I was going to. Hard and long.

Date must have been the magic word because Penny Jo let go of him and put her hands on her hips. "Oh. You mean like in the North Pole?"

I nodded.

She shrugged. "Y'all can have that cold weather. I hate it." Then she flounced off.

I stared at Cooper, not quite sure whether I had the words for what had just happened. I took a long drink of my wine.

He laughed. "She's a fun one, huh?"

"Let's deliver these drinks and go for a little walk."

"You sure you want to leave Sanders by himself?"

"He's a big boy, he'll be fine for a few minutes. Besides, Olive's keeping an eye on him. Trust me."

"You got it." He took the beer back from me and went to hand them off, then rejoined me. "Where to, Your Highness?"

"I don't know. But away from the crowd for a bit."

"I know a spot." He offered me his arm.

I took it, and he walked me around the room and outside onto a large patio area. The moon cast the garden in a silvery light that almost looked like snow. "Oh, this is so pretty."

"I thought you'd like it."

I leaned on the railing, closed my eyes and inhaled. The autumn air was crisp with the promise of colder nights to come. My kind of weather. I looked at him. "I like it very much."

He stepped in behind me, putting his hands next to mine on the railing. He leaned in to kiss the soft spot behind my ear. I shivered for a reason that had nothing to do with the temperature. "I'd offer to warm you up, but I know you like the cold."

I laughed and twisted to face him, slipping my arms around his neck. "Thank you for defending my royal honor earlier."

He smiled, sly and sweet. "I thought Penny Jo ought to know who she was dealing with."

"I owe you. And I'd like to pay now." I pressed

my mouth to his and kissed him just as long and hard as I'd wanted to a few minutes ago.

His hands left the railing to settle on my lower back. He pulled me closer and his warmth spread though me in delicious waves.

A moment more, and I broke the kiss to lean back and gaze up at him. The music inside changed to a soft, pretty waltz.

Cooper paced back, his hands out. "Shall we?"

I stepped into his embrace and we started to dance, slowly twirling around in the evening air. It was perfect.

"The clock is about to strike midnight for me," he whispered.

"I know," I answered, aware that even now Greyson was probably inside looking for me. "Are you going to stay?"

"And watch the vampire dance with you? I'll pass."

I sighed. "Good. I was afraid you'd stick around and dance with Penny Jo."

He snorted. "Actually, that's not a bad idea."

I lifted my head off his shoulder to shoot him a look. "Go ahead. She is kind of your type. The cheerleader to your quarterback."

He spun me out, twirled me, then brought me back in, chuckling. "Is that what you think? I'm wounded."

I loved this bantering we did. It made being with Cooper so easy.

One of the doors behind us opened and a throat cleared. "Sorry to interrupt the party, but you might want to get in here, Jayne."

We both turned to see Greyson standing there.

I kept hold of Cooper. "What's going on?"

Greyson smirked. "I think you could say the party just got its first crasher."

Cooper and I headed inside.

A small crowd had gathered near the far end of the ballroom with Sanders in its midst. Olive was at his side, naturally, but Elenora was there too. They were all watching a dark figure approaching.

A woman. Beautiful, but so thin that 'skeletal' was the only word I could think of. Jet hair, obsidian eyes, and a long black dress that seemed to be made of smoke and fog as much as fabric. Raven feathers and small bones decorated her hair, and around her waist, on an onyx silk cord, hung two interesting items. The first was an hourglass very much like the one Sanders wore. Except this one was black. Even the glittering sand inside looked like tiny ebony diamonds. The second was a wicked-looking curved blade with a short hilt. I didn't want to think about what she used that for.

The deeper into the room she traveled, the more heads turned. The dancers kept moving but their routes slowed to maintain their vantage points.

The three of us joined the group around Sanders, but we stayed at the edge. Closest to the woman.

Beside me, Greyson touched one of the necklaces he wore and whispered a few words I couldn't make out. They sounded very much like a spell of protection.

The woman stopped at the perimeter of the crowd

and smiled. "Hello, Tempus." Her voice held a quietness I hadn't expected.

He hesitated, then made a small, discontented noise. "Luna."

She jerked her head. The movement seemed birdlike somehow. "You don't look happy to see me. I thought we were beyond that."

His eyes held suspicion. "Why are you here?"

She stepped back, clearly surprised. "I heard about your book. I wanted to wish you well. Show my support."

His expression softened. "That's very kind of you."

I glanced at Olive. She was bristled up like a wet hen. Who was this woman?

Luna nodded. "I thought I might come to the signing tomorrow. Get a copy for myself." She gestured with one hand, her fingers thin as twigs. "If that's all right with you."

Sanders nodded. "Yes, of course."

Elenora waved at the musicians and the music picked up, a livelier tune than the dirge it had devolved into.

Luna tipped her head again, listening and smiling. Then her expression turned coy and she extended her hand toward Sanders. "A dance for old times' sake?"

Sanders opened his mouth as if to answer, then closed it, took a deep breath, and accepted Luna's hand. As the odd pair made their way onto the dance floor, the party seemed to normalize. More couples joined them and the conversation levels returned to a soft, indecipherable hum.

"Who is that woman? Luna who?" I whispered to Coop and Greyson.

"No clue," Cooper said.

"Me either," Greyson added.

Olive stepped up beside us. "That's Luna Nyx." Her lip practically curled with distaste. "Mistress of Nightmares. And Tempus' ex-wife."

Neither Cooper, Greyson or I said a word for a long minute. I think we were just absorbing it. First of all, that Sanders had been married. Secondly, that he'd been married to the woman he was now dancing with. And thirdly, that she was in charge of nightmares. Actually, that part wasn't so hard to believe.

I couldn't help but wonder if her presence in town was what had caused my and Cooper's nightmares. Was that something she could control? Or did they just follow her like a dark cloud, raining on anyone unlucky enough to be underneath?

Greyson finally spoke. "I take it the split was amicable?"

Olive made a grumbly noise. "Not that he led me to believe. But she came out of the marriage with more than she went in with. The power of nightmares. Between us, Sanders was happy to let them go. Nightmares have never been his thing."

I glanced at her. "So you thought they weren't friends? They sure look chummy enough now."

And they did, waltzing around on the dance floor, talking, smiling. If they didn't get on, they were doing a stellar job of hiding it.

"I don't trust her," Olive groused. "I don't know what her game is, but I don't like that she's here. Or that she's coming to the signing tomorrow."

I wanted to pat Olive on the shoulder, to comfort her, but she didn't look like she was in any mood to be touched. "I promise, we'll keep an eye out tomorrow. If she does stop by to get a book, I'll personally do whatever I can to see that's all she does."

Olive took a deep breath, then nodded. "Thank you. But if Lunatic Luna Nyx wants to cause trouble, no one's going to stop her."

Cooper shot me a side glance as if to say no one was going to stop Olive from thinking that way, either.

I gave him a subtle nod in return.

Then he turned toward Olive and held out his hand. "How about a turn around the floor, Miss Pine?"

Olive's mouth came open in surprise, but her hand reached out for Cooper's. He whisked her off before she could say a word.

Greyson moved closer to me. "Gotta give elfboy his due. Way to take one for the team."

"Oh, behave. Olive's not so bad."

"No." He smiled at me. "But she's no Jayne Frost." He took my hand. "Shall we?"

"Might as well. I wouldn't mind getting a close-up look at Luna either, so dance me in that direction."

"Feeling brave, eh?"

"Just curious."

He did as I asked and I tried to be as shrewd as possible as we moved closer to Sanders' ex, but there was quite a bit of distance between them and the rest of the dancers. Like they had an invisible force field around them.

And when I got close enough, I could see why. Tiny spiders and shiny black beetles crawled through Luna's hair. The seams of her dress appeared to occasionally open and close like tiny, hungry mouths. And her skin was so pale that the veins beneath were a blue, pulsating map.

I couldn't imagine a more perfect person to be the Mistress of Nightmares.

I might have also gasped.

Greyson, probably sensing my discomfort, danced us in the other direction. I stared at his chest, trying to put a new image in my head. He wasn't in a tuxedo, but in one of his many velvet frock coats (this one midnight blue), which he'd matched up with a pair of leather pants and a lacy black shirt.

"You okay?" he asked.

I nodded and smiled weakly. "I just wasn't prepared for that."

"No one ever is. Prepared for a nightmare, that is." He rubbed his thumb on the back of my hand.

"True." But Luna was still a curiosity to me. She had to be an elemental. The fact that I'd never met her before meant nothing. There were certainly plenty of elementals I'd never met. And my guess was, Luna didn't exactly get invited to a lot of parties. "I'm surprised Elenora let her in."

"Elenora probably had no idea she was coming." Greyson checked the crowd around us, perhaps for the vampire herself, before he spoke. "In fact, Luna doesn't register."

"What do you mean?"

"Vampire senses are extremely acute. With minimal effort, I can hear your heart beating even over the noise of this party. With a little more effort, I can pick out the heartbeat of just about anyone else in this room. Anyone who has a heartbeat, that is." He glanced at Sanders. "Luna does not. In fact, it's like she doesn't even exist. If I try to focus on only her, there's nothing but a black hole there."

"Wow."

He nodded. "Whatever her powers are, I'd say they're more than anyone knows. I think Olive is right. You should be wary of her. Maybe she has just come to buy a book and show her support. But if she hasn't…" He shrugged.

Snowballs.

As much as I hated to cut this night short, I needed to talk to my dad. Now. This event with Sanders could *not* go sideways. Not after the great day we'd had today. I sighed.

Greyson smiled a little sadly. "Come on, I'll take you home."

Since Cooper hadn't left yet, I told him my suspicions and that I was going home to talk to my dad about them. I didn't want him to think I was ditching early on account of Greyson arriving. But Cooper unexpectedly volunteered to stay and keep an eye on Luna and Sanders. I kissed him for that, right in front of Greyson and everything.

The vampire didn't seem too bothered by it, which was nice. I had enough to deal with. In fact, we were almost to my place (his '69 Camaro can move) when I realized I'd barely said anything to him. I'd been staring out at the night, wrapped up in what-ifs. I looked at him. "Sorry for being so quiet. I really appreciate you taking me home."

"Happy to help."

"I know it meant cutting our time at the party short." Sweet fancy Christmas, he was pretty. How was I ever going to decide between him and Cooper? "I'll make it up to you when this whole thing is over."

He grinned as he pulled onto my street. "I'll take

that. Not that there's really anything for you to make up. Life happens, lass."

"Very kind of you."

He parked outside the warehouse door and turned the car off. "Besides, who says the night has to end? Call your dad, fill him in, and then let's see what happens next. We can always get some Salvatore's and hang out."

"True. I never did get anything to eat at the party." I reached for the door handle.

He held up a finger. "Just a sec."

Almost quicker than my elven eyes could follow, he was out of the car, around to my side, and opening the door. His vampire speed really was something. "There you go."

I took the hand he offered and let him help me out. "Thank you."

He didn't release my hand. Instead he shut the door and pulled me closer. "I don't think I've told you yet this evening how absolutely stunning you look."

I smiled. "We *were* a little distracted by Sanders' ex."

"I hate that another woman kept me from telling you how beautiful you look. Or from doing this." He leaned in, his eyes glowing with that very distinct vampire light, and kissed me. His spicy cinnamon scent surrounded me as his hands went to my hips, putting us in more intimate contact.

I swear I felt the tiniest scrape of his fangs on my bottom lip.

Just when my knees went weak, he stepped away. The kiss couldn't have lasted more than a few seconds, and I wasn't ready for it to be over. But work awaited. With a sigh, I pulled my keys out and got us into the building. A minute later, we walked into my apartment.

Well, I walked in. Greyson hung back by the door. "How about I run down to Salvatore's and pick something up? Give you a chance to talk to your dad alone."

That wasn't entirely necessary, but it would be easier. "Thanks, that would be great. You know what I like."

He grinned and wiggled his brows. "Yes, I do."

I laughed as he left, happy for the moment of levity before I had to get serious. I sat on the couch, picked up the snow globe from the side table, and gave it a shake. I set it on the coffee table, watching the snow whirl and wondering what my dad was doing.

Spider wandered in, yawning, and flopped down at my feet. I bent to scratch his tummy. "How's it going, Spidercat?"

"Sleepy. Hungry." He stretched to expose more of his belly to my fingers. "Mama scratch Spider more."

"That's pretty much the story of your life, isn't it? I'll feed you in a few minutes, okay?"

"Kay." He closed his eyes and started purring as he curled around my left foot.

My dad's face appeared in the snow. "Hi, sweetheart. Don't you look beautiful? Your mom is going to be mad she missed you, but she and your aunt Martha are going over the Christmas lunch menu with the caterers."

"That's a big job." Christmas lunch was shared by all of the company's workers. So basically, it was like the entire North Pole eating together. Fortunately, the catering staff had their own brand of magic. "Tell them I said hi and I'll send a picture when I get a chance."

"Will do. I guess you're home from the party now. I thought you'd be there longer. How did the signing go today? I'm guessing good, judging by the fact that you had me send more books midway through."

"It was amazing." I filled him in on the details and gave him the day's numbers.

"Wow." He sat back, shaking his head. "That's outstanding."

"It is…really, really good."

His brows narrowed. "But?"

I grimaced. "There's a reason I'm home early. Do you know who Luna Nyx is?"

He nodded, his expression growing serious. "Yes. Sanders' ex-wife. She's also the Mistress of Nightmares. She was a working reaper before she met him, though. That's how she met him, but that's a story for another time. Being the Mistress of Nightmares, that came later. She got that power in the divorce, actually."

"How are the nightmares controlled?"

"She's got an hourglass just like Sanders'. Much darker magic, obviously."

That was the hourglass I'd seen swinging at her waist.

My dad went on. "Although frankly, I think Sanders was happy to give the nightmares up. That was never his bag."

I nodded. That matched up with what Olive had said.

He laughed softly. "Way more than you wanted to know, probably."

"Actually, it's not." And the reaper thing made total sense, having seen her. "How do you know so much about her?"

"I'm the Winter King. It's my job to know about things like the elementals. The full-blooded ones are certainly a unique variety of elf." He shrugged. "We've never had a problem with one. Maybe because your uncle bridges the gap between us. But knowledge is power when you're the one in charge. You'll see."

"I guess." But that time was so far in the future it was hard to imagine.

"So what's up? Why the questions?"

I took a breath. "Luna showed up at the party tonight. Uninvited, in case that needs to be said."

Ice vapor curled out of my father's nose and mouth, a sure sign that he wasn't happy. "She showed up."

I nodded. "She didn't really cause any problems. She said she was just in town to support Sanders' book launch. In fact, they ended up dancing together." I shrugged. "Seemed pretty chummy to me."

Spider got up and trotted off somewhere.

My dad steepled his fingers together and shifted in his chair. "But you wouldn't be calling me if you didn't think there was a potential for trouble."

"Yeah." I leaned forward, putting my elbows on

my knees. "I've had two nightmares in the last twenty-four hours and I know someone else who's had one. I'm not saying Luna's the cause—I don't even know when she arrived in town—but it's sort of coincidental that on the night the Sandman arrives, my dreams go dark."

"Agreed."

"If she is here to create problems...well, we can't have that. And I don't know what to do about it. Plus, Olive, Sanders' assistant, seemed pretty sure that Luna was up to no good." I exhaled. "Or could be."

"She's a powerful woman. Luna," my dad corrected himself, "not Olive. As a former reaper, she literally has the power of life and death in her hands. And the power to cause fear? That's no small thing either."

She wasn't exactly warm and cuddly in person either. "But she can't control Sanders, can she? What could she do to him? Give him nightmares?"

My dad paused for a beat. "I don't think so, but I don't know for sure. Most elementals are a curious and powerful breed, Jay. Uncle Kris is proof of that."

I loved my uncle, but my dad was right. Uncle Kris had his idiosyncrasies. "That's what worries me. Is there anything I can do? Any way to prevent her from causing trouble?"

"I don't know. Let me talk to Kris and I'll get back to you in the morning. In fact, call me when you get into the office. That should give your uncle and me a chance to come up with something. Kris knows them both better than I do so he should be able to offer some help."

"Thanks. I'll talk to you in the morning, then."

"Be safe, sweetheart. Love you."

"Love you, too."

The snow stopped swirling. I sat back and tipped my head onto the back of the couch so I could stare at the ceiling for a moment. My life. Never a dull moment.

I got up to change out of my dress and heels, but I'd only just thrown on yoga pants and an oversized sweatshirt when there was a knock at the door. I checked the peephole, but I already knew it was Greyson. I could smell the pizza.

I opened the door. "That was fast."

He walked in carrying the pizza box and a plastic bag. "I didn't want it to get cold. Everything good?"

"I don't know. I guess. Let's eat and I'll fill you in."

He gave me a quick once-over. "I like the tiara with the casual look. The princess at home."

I reached up and felt the crown still perched on my head. "I totally forgot I was still wearing it." I eased it loose, pulling free a few strands of hair from my twist. Juniper had done an excellent job of securing that tiara in place. I put the diamond crown back in its box, then ran to the bathroom, brushed out my hair and scraped it into a quick ponytail. The make-up I'd take off later.

Right now, pizza.

Greyson had put the box on the coffee table, and had unpacked the Salvatore's bag to add a stack of paper napkins, packets of hot pepper flakes, parmesan and two paper plates. "This all right? Or should I take it to the kitchen?"

"No, this is great." I sat with him on the couch, crossing my legs. It had been fun to get dressed up, but it was good to be in comfy clothes again.

He opened the box and we each grabbed a slice. As we ate, I filled him in on what my dad had said.

Greyson swallowed the bite he'd just taken. "I must admit, I know very little about elementals. I didn't even know they were a kind of elf. I thought reapers were reapers, Santa Claus was a winter elf and the Sandman was just the Sandman."

"Most people, I mean, most supernaturals don't know much about them. It's rare that you'll find an elf who will discuss them since they're such a secret group. Elementals usually just identify with those they've surrounded themselves with."

"Like your uncle and the winter elves."

"Yes. But he is part winter elf. So that's not entirely wrong." I reached for another slice. "And really, very few supernaturals ever run into an elemental. They don't really mix."

"Which is why Sanders' trip here is causing you stress."

"That's part of it, yes. I mean, can you imagine if, the first time he's decided to venture into the human world, something goes wrong and I could have prevented it?" I exhaled a long breath. "Not good. For me or the store."

Greyson tossed the crust of the slice he'd just finished into the box. "It might be Sanders' first visit, but he isn't the first elemental to spend time in the mortal world. He can't be."

"No, he's not. I mean, there's my uncle. Well, he's really only here on Christmas Eve. I don't think you can count that. And he does his best not to be seen."

"That's not who I was thinking about." He leaned down to scratch Spider, who'd just walked in and sat by Greyson.

"Who then? Tell me."

"Are all reapers elementals?"

"Yes. It's what they are."

He opened his mouth, then closed it again. "I'm telling you this in the strictest confidence."

"Understood." Now I was really curious.

"The supernatural who owns Insomnia, the night-club where we met, is a reaper. Retired reaper, technically. At least I think he's retired. Anyway, he's lived here in Nocturne Falls for a while now."

"Wow. And you know him?"

"Yes. Not well. He keeps to himself. But I've done a few things for him." Greyson shrugged. "Decent guy. Very quiet. A little dark, but then that's not so unusual considering who he is."

"Is he…like Luna? Thin and goth-looking? Does he have spiders in his hair?"

Greyson choked on a bite of pizza. "Not that I'm aware of."

"Well, she did."

He peered at me. "Are you sure? I don't know about that. Maybe that was her way of…dressing up?"

"If so, um, ew. The only spider I like is that little black fluffball sitting at your feet." Spider trilled at me. I smiled, then finished my slice and tossed the crust in the box next to Greyson's. "I guess I should go to bed. Tomorrow is another long day and I have to be on my game in case Luna tries anything."

"Of course." Greyson stood. "Do you want me to come by the store tomorrow? Just in case? Seeing as how I'm technically already dead there isn't anything Luna can do to me."

I blinked at him. "Well, that just filled my head with all sorts of awful new possibilities. Do you think she'd do that? Go all 'grim reaper, I'm here for your soul' on me?"

"No. I'm sure all she's going to do is come by, get a book, and be on her way."

I frowned as I got to my feet. "Let's hope. Sure, if you want to swing by that might not be a bad idea. Signing is from three to five, one hour shorter than today's."

"I'll be there." He gave me a kiss, short and sweet, then headed for the door. "See you tomorrow. Pleasant dreams."

"That's the plan."

Thankfully, my sleep was uneventful. No better or worse than any other night and by morning, I felt about as rested as I usually did. I walked out to the kitchen, ready for the day but in need of some breakfast. After I fed Spider, naturally, because that's how the ranking went. Spider, then me.

The cat himself sat on the windowsill. It was one of his favorite spots to hang out in because it got sun and he could watch the people below. Right now, however, he was licking the back of one leg like that was his job. He paused to look at me and meow loudly.

I glanced at his bowl. It was empty. "I take it you're ready for breakfast?"

"Spider likes Chicken Party."

"I'm very aware—"

"*Miss Frost.*"

The bellow came from above me, loud enough to register clearly through the floors and distinct enough that I knew whose voice it was.

Sanders. And apparently, he needed me. For once, Spider was going to have to wait.

I didn't know what he wanted, but it didn't sound good from the sternness of his shout. I took off for the third floor, running the steps instead of waiting for the elevator and barreling down the hall until I was at his door. I knocked. "Mr. Sanders? It's Jayne. What's the—"

The door opened and a very angry Tempus scowled down at me. "My hourglass is gone."

Big hairy snowballs. A chill swept through me. I swallowed the sense of panic rising up in me. "Your hourglass is gone?"

He filled the door frame, casting me in shadow. "Did I stutter?"

"No, sir." The mountainous teddy bear of a man was gone, replaced by the hulking, surly elemental now before me. I don't know how I'd ever thought his size wasn't intimidating. It was *hugely* intimidating. "Do you have any idea where it might be?"

He leaned toward me, almost making me flinch. "If I had any idea where it was, do you think we'd be having this conversation?"

"No, sir." I straightened, pulling myself up to my full height. "We'll find it." I glanced past him as best I could. "Where's Olive? Is she already looking? If she's checking the apartment, I'll go out and retrace your steps."

"Olive went out to get my breakfast."

I nodded. I guess that explained why I was getting the full treatment. "All right, she can help us when she returns. Can I come in?"

The realization that I was still out in the hall seemed to placate him a bit. He backed up and let me in. The living room was in shambles with cushions pulled off the sofa and books knocked off the shelves. At least he'd done a little looking himself.

I closed the door behind me, not entirely comfortable with being alone and confined with him, but figured my status as a royal should be enough to keep me safe. "Where's the last place you saw it?"

"It was on its cord, attached to me. Where it always is." He glowered at me. "Do you understand how important this is, Miss Frost? No one touches my hourglass. No one but me."

"Absolutely, I—"

The door opened and Olive strode in, bags from Mummy's swinging from both hands. I should have told her they delivered. My mouth started to water at the scent of the blueberry pancakes and cinnamon rolls, and my traitorous stomach rumbled.

"Olive," I said loudly to cover the sound of my hunger. "I'm so glad you're back. Tempus has misplaced his hourglass—"

87

"I have not misplaced it," he roared. "It's been stolen. There's a thief in this town. In this building!"

"Whoa." I held up my hands. "You didn't say anything about it being stolen. Who do you think would have taken it?"

His gaze narrowed. "Who else? The woman who dared interrupt my party last night. The woman who—"

"Luna?" But they'd been so friendly.

"Yes," Olive said with a somewhat exasperated sigh. "I'm sure your ex-wife strolled in here and took it."

"Luna absolutely could have," he snarled.

Olive sighed again, then shook her head and pursed her mouth like she had better things to do. Bags in hand, she walked past him to the dining table, put the bags down, then marched into the back of the apartment where the bedrooms were.

"Olive, come back here," he yelled after her. "It's been stolen, I tell you. Stolen! We need to find out where Luna's staying and go talk to her immediately." He turned to me. "I never should have trusted that woman. Never. To think I almost bought her story about wanting to get back together."

Olive returned a few moments later to stand at the end of the hall. She crossed her arms and gave him a rather deliberate look. "It's under your bed."

He shifted, chewing on his lower lip. "You didn't touch it, did you?" His voice was distinctly lower.

"Do I ever?" she asked.

He didn't answer, just shuffled past her into the bedroom.

She sighed, uncrossed her arms and went to the table to start unpacking the food. She glanced at me. "I'm sorry about that. Happens every so often. And I'm always here to take care of it, except this time."

"Good thing you came back when you did." Whatever she was getting paid, it wasn't enough.

"Yes." She pulled box after box out of the takeout bags. "Would you like to stay for breakfast? There's more than enough."

Not for a cold second. "I've already eaten, thank you. Besides, I have to get to my office. Have to make sure we've got enough stock for the signing this afternoon. And I have a business call with my father this morning." I was so glad to have an excuse, I didn't even have to make myself smile. "Work is never done."

She returned the smile, but it looked strained. I understood. "That's for sure. We'll see you later, then."

I nodded. "Later."

I let myself out and got back to my apartment almost as quickly as I'd vacated it. I wondered if Kip and Juniper had heard the commotion on the first floor. The store had been open for about twenty minutes.

Rowley and his wife must have heard it. I glanced toward my ceiling. Their apartment was right across the hall from Sanders', directly above mine. Hopefully, they wouldn't call me up to explain because I did not want to risk running into Sanders again so soon. I needed a break from him. With that goal in mind, I fed Spider, then grabbed a foil pouch of toaster pastries, a

Dr Pepper, the box holding my tiara, and my purse—with my keys and phone in it—and went downstairs.

I tossed everything but the tiara box on my desk, then went to put that in the Santa's Bag. I stood there and waited until the bag went from full to empty so I knew it had safely arrived in the NP. With that done, I went back to my office.

Thankfully, there was a toaster in the employee breakroom. I stuck my cardboard pastries in there to try to bring them to life. Why did I eat these things? Because they were fast and sugary. Not because they tasted great, that's for sure.

They popped out and I used my magic to waft a little cold air over them so I didn't burn myself on the ridiculously hot frosting. I pinched them onto a paper plate and took them back to my office. I could have had a delicious Mummy's breakfast, but there was no way I could hang out with Sanders after that nonsense this morning.

He hadn't even apologized. I guess that was the temperamental bit my dad had mentioned.

My dad!

Snowballs. I was supposed to call him. Sanders' outburst had really flustered me. I gave the globe a shake.

He showed up instantly. "Hey, there's my girl. How are you this morning, Jay?"

"Okay, considering Sanders had a little diva fit after misplacing his hourglass."

My dad's eyes widened. "Everything good now?"

"Seems to be." I took a sip of my Dr Pepper. "So what did you find out about dealing with Luna? You and Uncle Kris come up with anything?"

"Not much. Your uncle just confirmed what I already suspected. We don't know the full extent of her powers. Like most elementals. Which means she could be a huge threat, or none at all. And because the reaper ranks are so closed, we don't know much about her life before Sanders either. Sorry this isn't any help. Your uncle thinks that if Luna shows up, you should take her aside and talk to her."

"Oh, awesome. I was hoping I'd get to have a delicate conversation with a potentially fatal supernatural today."

"Jayne, she won't hurt you. That would be a huge escalation. She'd be taking on the entire North Pole if she did that. No, if she's going to do anything, it'll be directed at Sanders."

I gave my dad my best skeptical look. "And you think she's just going to tell me what her plans are if I ask nicely?"

"Maybe." He hesitated. "Just be friendly. Maybe chat her up a bit. See what her mood is like. You know."

"And if I think she's there to cause trouble? Or to try to hurt Sanders?"

My father's mouth flattened into a thin, hard line. "Then you have authorization to take her into the warehouse and freeze her solid."

"What?"

He nodded. "If it comes to that, notify us as soon as you're done, and your uncle and I will come down there."

"And what, I'm supposed to just keep her on ice

for the day and a half it takes you to get here?"

"We'll take the sleigh. You won't have to wait long."

I stared at him for a few seconds, mulling this whole thing over. "You really think it's going to come to that?"

"We hope not, but Sanders must be protected. Yes, he's a handful at times, but he provides the world with a very valuable service: sleep. We need him happy and healthy. The whole world does."

"But no pressure," I muttered to myself.

"I heard that," my dad said. "Listen, Jay, we're not leaving you to do this alone. That's why we said we'd come down there."

"I know. But wow."

He nodded. "I get it. I do."

"Okay. But I really hope she's just here to get a book."

"Us, too. Truly."

I took a breath and changed the subject. "Speaking of, two more things. I need the books for today."

"I already sent them through the Santa's Bag this morning. Didn't you get them?"

"Kip must have unloaded them already. I haven't been in the store yet, but I'll do that next. Also, I sent my tiara back this morning."

"Yes, I got a message from Heirlooms and Antiquities right before you called that it had been received and would be returned to the vaults shortly."

"Good. And as much as I love chatting with you, I should probably get to work."

"You should probably go get yourself a real breakfast. I see what you're eating. That's not going to do you any good with the day you have in front of you."

I laughed. "Is that an order?"

He smiled. "That's a royal decree. Go eat something substantial. Pancakes, waffles, some bacon, hash browns. They must have a decent breakfast place in that town."

"Oh, they do."

"Then I expect you to be there shortly after we hang up."

"Yes, King Dad. But first I need to make sure Kip took care of those books. Which I'm sure he did, but I still need to be in the store for a few minutes. That is what you pay me for."

"All right. But immediately after that, go eat."

"I will. I promise. Did Mom and Aunt Martha get everything settled with the caterers?"

"Not yet, but they're close. And I'd put your mother on, but you can talk to her tonight. I know what a busy day you have in front of you and she'll want to talk to you for an hour."

"Okay, but tell her I said hi."

"I will. Love you, Jay."

"Love you, Dad."

As the snow settled at the bottom of the globe, I tossed the toaster pastries in the trash. Then I sent Cooper a text about meeting me at Mummy's for breakfast. First of all because I owed him after he'd stayed at the party last night. Secondly, I wanted to know how the rest of the evening had gone between Luna and Sanders. And thirdly, eating there instead of ordering delivery meant I could have a little temporary distance from Sanders.

While I waited for Coop to get back to me, I went into the shop. There were a few customers, but nothing crazy. That would come later, most likely. Kip had the book display by the door looking great.

Juniper walked up as I was checking it out. "How was last night? Did you have fun?" She grinned. "Are you hungover?"

"Not even slightly. It was a weird evening. And a short one. Sanders' ex-wife showed up."

Her eyes went round. "What? Tell me everything."

I did, right down to the detail about the spiders in her hair.

"Ew," Juniper shuddered. "And he was married to her? What kind of a guy looks at a chick that arachno-friendly and thinks, 'I gotta get me some of that'?"

"Apparently, the Sandman does. But look, if she does come by the shop today, we have to be super nice and totally normal to her. We do not want to set her off."

"I hear that. I'll make sure Kip and the rest of the crew know."

"Thanks. I'm going to be out for a bit. I need to eat something. My dad's making me go eat, actually."

"You have to obey if it's a royal decree." She laughed.

"Exactly." My phone buzzed. Probably Cooper. "I'm going to run. Call me if you need me."

"I will. Enjoy your breakfast."

I checked the message as I returned to my office. Cooper couldn't make it to breakfast (bummer) because he was on duty at the fire house, but said nothing weird had happened between Sanders and Luna the rest of the night. Just some small talk and a little more dancing. All very friendly.

That might have been, but Sanders sure had been quick to conclude that Luna was behind his missing hourglass. That got me thinking about what Greyson had told me last night. There was another reaper in town.

I sent Greyson a quick text with my new idea and asked him to join me for breakfast.

He answered as I was walking into Mummy's. *Can't do breakfast but I can make the rest happen. Pick you up at the warehouse in an hour.*

I might be alone for breakfast, but that was okay. The rest of my morning was about to get really interesting. Maybe I'd just eat in my office. I went to the take-out counter, ready to place an order, when I felt a hand on my arm.

"Princess. I mean, Jayne." Birdie Caruthers grinned at me. "How are you?"

"I'm doing all right. How are you, Birdie?"

"Oh, I'm fine. Worked to the bone by that nephew of mine. That's why I'm here. Getting some cinnamon rolls." She leaned in. "He's a little stressed with the baby's due date getting closer. Needed some comfort food, you know how it is."

I nodded. "That's right, I forgot his wife is about to have a baby." I knew the sheriff had adopted Ivy's son, but this was their first child together. "How exciting! I guess I won't be seeing Ivy at Delaney's Delectables much longer." The last time I'd been in Delaney's shop, Ivy had been showing pretty well.

"No, she'll be off on maternity leave. And between us, probably won't return to work. I think she's just going to stay home and be a full time mama. But Delaney's already got some new people lined up to cover the shifts." Birdie tipped her head, eyes lively. "Hey, are you in a rush?"

"Not for an hour. Why?"

"We should get a cup of coffee and catch up."

"I was actually going to get breakfast. I haven't eaten yet and I'm starving."

Birdie grinned. "Now that you mention it, I could go for some eggs Benedict." She waved at a passing waitress. "Lynette, we're going to take that table over there."

Lynette nodded at us. "I'll be right over with menus."

Birdie was never dull company, so it turned out I'd been right on the money when I imagined my morning getting more interesting.

Greyson was right on time to pick me up. Unfortunately, I wasn't ready. Breakfast with Birdie had gone a little longer than I'd intended (Penny Jo *may* have come up) and I'd had to hustle to get back to the warehouse. Even with that hustle, I was a few minutes late.

He was leaning against the wall near the warehouse door, a few feet from where his Camaro was parked curbside. And of course, he looked perfect. Kind of rakish and very bad-boy in black jeans, leather jacket, and Ray-Bans.

I waved as I approached. "Sorry. I know I'm late. I ran into Birdie at Mummy's and—"

Greyson laughed. "That's really all the explanation I need." He straightened. "Do you need to go in or can we just leave from here?"

"Maybe…" If something else had come up Olive or Juniper would have texted me. I checked my phone anyway just to be sure I hadn't missed anything. I hadn't. Big relief there. "No, we can leave from here."

"Great." He opened my car door, waited for me to get in to close it again, then went around and slid behind the wheel.

I put my seat belt on—a lap belt only, because in 1969 safety was not their first concern. "I need to send a quick text, then you can fill me in on whatever I need to know."

He nodded and pulled into traffic.

I shot Juniper a note. *Off on an errand, back in a bit. Text if you need me.* Then I put my phone in my purse. "So. We're going to see the reaper. That sounds so ominous. What should I know?"

"Just one thing that I can think of. Well, two things. Don't touch him. And don't talk about him afterward."

"Wow, ominous indeed. Why can't I touch him? Or talk about him? Not that I'm going to do either. Just curious."

Greyson slanted his eyes at me. "Don't talk about him because he likes his anonymity. And the reason you can't touch him is that he retired because he can't control his ability to reap souls. Which means his touch is deadly. Sometimes."

My brows lifted. "Only sometimes. That's reassuring."

Greyson sighed. "I'm serious about not saying a word about this to anyone. I've been sworn to secrecy as well. The only reason Lucien's even seeing you is because he knows Luna."

"Lucien? Do all reapers have names that start with L? Lily would be a good reaper name, seeing as how that's a funeral flower and all."

"Jayne." Greyson's tone held an edge. "I realize you're hyped up on sugar and breakfast with Birdie, but this is serious business."

I narrowed my eyes. "I know it's serious. Last night, a woman with the powers of death and fear showed up and announced she's coming to my store today. During what could potentially be one of the busiest afternoons we've ever had. Then I had my head chewed off this morning by the elemental who controls the world's sleep, because he misplaced his most valuable tool. And now you're taking me to see a being who could kill me with his touch? Excuse me if I use snark as a defense. I'm a little stressed. I'd rather laugh than cry."

Greyson reached out and took my hand. "I'm sorry. I know this is a lot for anyone to handle. But you don't have to handle it alone. I'm here whenever you need me. *Anything* you need, just ask. I told you I'd come to the store today and help. What else can I do?"

I let out a long breath and tried to relax my shoulders, which had somehow gotten bunched up around my ears. "Having you at the store will be a big help. That's really all I can think of right now. Everything else...I'll just deal with as it comes."

He squeezed my hand. "It's all going to be okay."

"I hope so." We rode in silence for a few moments before a new thought entered my head. "So Lucien's touch won't affect you?"

"No. I'm already dead. He can't kill me twice."

"That's why he's had you do work for him. No worries about accidentally reaping you. What kind of stuff have you done for him?"

"Errands. Bigger things than his housemate could manage. Some business stuff for the club."

My forehead wrinkled. "Back up. Death has a roommate?"

"Sort of. She's a ghost. Kind of. The last soul he reaped. And the first one that was accidental. Anyway, he was able to give her back her soul, but the damage was done. The death part was permanent. So now she's a ghost with the ability to become corporeal enough to do things like get groceries, run to the post office, and see a movie now and then."

I stared at Greyson for a full minute. "You're serious."

"As a heart attack."

I slipped down in my seat. "Sweet Christmas crackers, this town is weird." Then I sat up again. "Do I get to meet this ghost?"

He nodded. "I'm sure Hattie will be there. She always is."

"Why does she stay with Lucien? I mean, if he's the one who offed her and everything…" I wouldn't stick around the guy who killed me. Even if it *was* accidental.

Greyson stared out through the windshield. "Lucien is her grandson."

"Oh." A wave of sadness washed through me and I instantly understood more about Lucien than I could have imagined. It took a second before I could say anything. "That's kind of awful. But sweet too, that she's stayed with him."

Greyson nodded as he pulled into the parking lot

of Insomnia. "It is. Part of me is a little jealous that he gets to have a family member with him for eternity. And part of me can't imagine what it must feel like to know you accidentally cut short the life of someone you love."

"Wow. Yeah, that part would undo me, I think."

"It has him, too. You see why he wants to be left alone?"

"I do. Poor guy. But why call her his housemate? Why not just say Grandmother?"

"He doesn't like the reminder."

"I guess I can understand that." I stared at the old Caldwell Manufacturing building. Faded paint spelled out the name on the crumbling brick structure. If I didn't know better, I'd think the place was abandoned, not home to the hottest supernaturals-only nightclub in town. "So he lives in the same building as the club?"

Greyson nodded. "Yes. Ready to meet him?"

"I don't know. But I'm ready to find out more about Luna." I opened my own door this time.

We walked in together. There was no bouncer by the elevator like there had been the first night I'd come here, but the rest of the place looked the same. Dusty rows of machinery and worktables that spoke of the building's past stood in silent lines, and a dank, metallic smell hung in the air. Faint, but there.

Not a single indicator that this place housed a nightclub. Except for the shiny steel elevator against the far wall. That was a little out of place.

We went up to it and Greyson punched a code into the keypad. "Don't tell anyone I know how to access this elevator either."

"I won't."

The doors opened and we got on. He tapped the only button on the panel and down we went.

The elevator took us to the club level, but it looked nothing like it normally did. There were no drifts of manufactured fog, no cool blue lights, no walls of running water. All of that was turned off. It still had the sleek, industrial thing happening, and the same white leather furniture and floaty drapery, but without the razzle-dazzle of the extras and the crowds of beautiful people, it seemed like a much more ordinary place than I remembered.

"This way," Greyson said. He pressed on one of the walls next to the elevator. And it opened.

He pushed it wide. It was a hallway. A nice one. Could have been in any upscale house in the town with its hardwood floors and wide moldings. The light was a little on the dim side, but considering we were underground, maybe it was just the lack of windows. Greyson cleared his throat and called out, "Lucien, we're here."

I had a feeling he already knew.

A short, slender woman with more silver than brunette in her hair appeared at the end of the hall. She wore a half-apron over her housedress, and her face bore the lines of someone who'd seen quite a few years.

Also, she was transparent. Literally see-through. I tried not to stare but I'd never seen a real ghost before. "Greyson, how nice to see you. And this must be the woman you spoke of. Come in."

Greyson walked through so I followed. "Hi, Hattie. Yes, this is Jayne." He turned to me. "Jayne, this is Hattie Dupree. Lucien's housemate."

And grandmother. "Nice to meet you." I stuck my hand out on instinct. It was what you did, after all. But even as my muscles moved, I knew she couldn't shake my hand. How could she? She wasn't solid.

But right before my eyes, that changed. I could no longer see the walls and floor behind her. And then her hand shook mine, just as warm and substantial as any living person. The look on my face must have summed up my thoughts.

She laughed. "Not what you were expecting, I imagine. Most people don't know what meeting a ghost will be like." Her smile was infectious. "I have to tell you, you still don't know. I'm not like most ghosts. I can take on a solid form. They can't all do that, from what I understand. Take Gertrude, who lives in the Van Zant's attic. She can't do corporeal. Real shame, too, because it would be nice to have a friend visit now and then that Lucien wouldn't mind."

I had no idea what to say, or who Gertrude was. So I just nodded and smiled.

Thankfully, Greyson stepped in. "Is Lucien here? He was expecting us."

"Yes, he's in his study. Let me take you into his parlor and then I'll let him know you're here."

"Thank you." Greyson put his hand on the small of my back, urging me ahead of him.

I followed Hattie. She was a nice lady and not the least bit scary for someone who was a ghost. The house—apartment, basement, whatever the right name for this place was—seemed like it had a lot of her touches in it. At least, I didn't think a reaper would be into lace doilies and dishes of hard candy, but then what did I know about reapers?

I was guessing Lucien didn't have anything to do with the smell of freshly baked bread, either.

She led us into a room that had none of the homey touches the rest of the place did. It was still nice—lots of dark wood paneling, leather furniture, and Oriental rugs. But there was something cold about it too. More like a doctor's waiting room than a parlor in some-one's home.

"Here you go," Hattie said. "I'll let him know you're here. Nice to meet you, Jayne."

"Nice to meet you, too, Hattie."

With a nod, she left.

The room seemed even colder with her gone. Greyson and I took a seat on the sofa, a big leather thing trimmed in upholstery nails. It wasn't nearly as comfortable as it looked.

I glanced at Greyson and raised my eyebrows, silently asking him, What next?

We wait, he mouthed back.

I sighed and leaned against the armrest, which was too high to comfortably put my arm on.

The temperature in the room dropped, which is a strange thing for me to notice. Winter elves don't have an issue with cold, as you can imagine. I looked at Greyson. "Did you feel that?"

But he was looking past me at the door.

I turned and saw a dark figure outlined in the

frame. I shuddered without meaning to, and instantly understood the chill.

Death had just joined us.

Luna hadn't made me feel this way, but then I'd met Luna in a room with several hundred other people. And she wasn't a working reaper anymore. But Greyson had said Lucien was retired.

Maybe it was his inability to control his reaping power. Maybe it was that flux in his system spilling off him. Whatever the reason, the whole vibe was creepy.

I wanted to retreat. To run. To hide behind Greyson.

I did none of those things, but I wanted to so badly that my nervous energy was more than I could contain.

Snow started falling in the room.

Lucien looked up. "I must say, I did not expect that."

"Jayne," Greyson said softly.

"Sorry," I muttered, deciding quickly to go with brutal honesty. "I'm a little nervous about meeting you. It'll stop in a second."

I closed my eyes, took a few deep breaths and wrestled hold of my self-control. Now was not the time or place to break out the shimmer. When I opened my eyes again, the snow was gone.

And Lucien was in front of me. Not within touching distance, but closer than he'd been before. "I don't mean to frighten you, Miss Frost, but I'm not a fool. I understand why my presence makes you feel that way. And I don't blame you."

He moved past me to sit in a wingback chair on the other side of the room. A much safer distance, in my opinion, but it made me sad for him.

He must have been a handsome man at one time. I could see traces of it in his face, but there was a gloom about him that made him look tired and worn. It came from his life, no doubt. And his trouble with his power.

Something living with Hattie must remind him of every day.

Greyson and I took our seats again now that Lucien was sitting too.

He leaned back and crossed one leg over the other. "Greyson tells me Luna Nyx is in town."

I nodded, happy to talk about the reason we'd come. "She is. I don't know when she arrived but she showed up at the party at Elenora Ellingham's last night. Luna claims she'll be stopping by my store today to see Tempus Sanders, the Sandman—"

"I know him," Lucien said.

"Well, he's doing a book signing there today. It's a kid's book, but Luna said she was going to come by and get a copy. To show her support."

"And you don't believe her."

"I don't know if I do or not. She didn't seem like she meant Sanders any ill-will, but there was a small incident this morning and he was instantly ready to blame her for it. It had nothing to do with her, as it turned out, but the fact that he so readily felt like she'd be behind something that would cause him trouble was a little unsettling. Oh, and his assistant seems to think Luna is trouble, too."

Lucien nodded. "She could be."

"Can you elaborate on that? Greyson said you know her."

"I knew of her. We were in different divisions." He shifted in his seat. "The reaper ranks are tightly closed, Miss Frost. Nothing about what we do or how we do it is ever to be shared."

"I understand. My family has its secrets too."

He smiled, which did wonders for his face. "Kris Kringle is your uncle."

It was a statement, not a question, but I answered anyway. "Yes."

Lucien spread his fingers over the arm of the chair. "Your family ties to the elemental are the only reason I agreed to see you." He hesitated. "And the only reason I am going to tell you what I think you need to know."

"What I need to know is Luna's weakness. How to prevent her from harming Sanders or disrupting the day. Can you tell me that?"

"I can tell you her weaknesses." He hesitated. "And how to defeat her, if necessary."

That was what I needed. "Thank you."

He held up a finger. "Don't thank me yet. You don't know my terms."

No, I didn't. And my nerves returned just wondering what they might be. "Can I hear them first before I agree?"

"Of course." He glanced at Greyson before continuing. "The information I am willing to give you, I am willing to give only to you. Greyson cannot be a part of this conversation. As much as I like Mr. Garrett, he is not an elemental nor does he have any elemental bloodlines."

Greyson lifted his hands. "I'm okay with leaving the room if that's what it takes."

But was I okay with being alone with Lucien? I guessed so. Sort of. I mean, if this is what it took, what choice did I have? I nodded my consent. "What else?"

"You will owe me a favor. To be called in at whatever time I see fit."

What sort of a favor could he want? "I don't know. I can't agree to anything that might be against the law, against my family, or cause harm to another person, or an animal. Be illegal in any way—"

Lucien laughed. "Miss Frost, I can only imagine what you think of me to guess my favor would result in any of those outcomes. I promise, it would be none of those things." He looked toward the door and sighed. "I might ask you to accompany Hattie somewhere."

"I'd be happy to spend time with her." That was easy.

"Or perhaps..." He glanced down at his lap. "I am isolated by choice, but there are times when I desire

109

company. Those times are rare, but they exist. And Greyson has graciously accepted many of my invitations. But I am a man, and the presence of a beautiful woman is something distinctly lacking in my home."

"You want me to find a woman to visit you?"

"I may want *you* to visit me." He raised his head, and smiled gently. "Perhaps that is not something you could agree to, knowing what you know about me. I understand. That was too much to ask. I assure you, I am not looking for anything beyond a meal or a conversation. I know you and Greyson are seeing each other."

A soft snarl spilled out of Greyson. I looked over. His eyes were lit from within, and his mouth bent in a grimace that exposed his fangs.

"Oh." Lucien jerked back, his expression growing horrified. "I see I did not make myself clear. I would like you *and* Greyson to visit or possibly join me for dinner."

I didn't think that's what Lucien had meant at all, but it got Greyson to relax. So much for him not being jealous. Or was he trying to protect me from Lucien? I turned to the reaper. "We could do that, definitely. But maybe you could wear gloves or something? You know, in case you have to pass me the salt or something."

His smile returned. "That would not be a problem. Thank you. Do you agree to my terms, then?"

Again, what choice did I have? "Yes, I agree."

Lucien looked at Greyson. "If you will give us a few minutes. I won't keep her long. Please shut the door on your way out."

Grudgingly, Greyson got up. He put his hand on my shoulder. "I'll be right outside, Jayne."

I patted his knuckles. "Thank you."

Once Greyson had left and the door was closed, Lucien began. "Reapers are assigned into divisions, and different reapers collect different kinds of souls. Luna was given a very difficult area. The criminally insane."

"And that affected her somehow?"

"It did. When we take a soul, that person's entire life passes through us."

I cringed. "Luna really had a tough go of it then."

He nodded. "She did. When she met Sanders, it changed everything for her. He made it possible for her to not only sleep peacefully, but to have pleasant dreams. For the first time since her assignment as a reaper of the criminally insane, she was able to put her job behind her."

"Wow. That must have been amazing for her."

"It was. And you can see how easy it was for her to fall in love with him."

"Absolutely."

"I tell you that just so you can understand her a little better."

I nodded. "Thank you. It definitely does that."

"If she is truly looking to hurt Sanders or ruin his day, there isn't much you can do to stop her. She's a very powerful elemental. But if it comes down to it, her weakness is the same as any reaper's."

I waited.

"Her scythe. Every reaper has one, active or not."

I inched toward the edge of my seat. "You mean the curved blade thing? She had one, a small one. It was hanging on her belt next to the black hourglass."

"That's her scythe. If you can take control of it, you will control her in a way." A muscle in his jaw twitched. "A reaper's scythe is the only way to kill a reaper."

I jerked back. "I don't want to kill her."

"But you may have to if your goal is to protect Sanders."

I bit my lip. This was way over my pay grade. And I was pretty sure my dad would agree with me. "Can't you tell this all to Greyson? Maybe he could be the one to—"

"No." Lucien's answer was a sharp, forceful bark. His face changed and I swear I saw a flash of a skull where his face had been. It was just for a second, but it *had* been there. "This information is never to be shared with anyone else. You agreed to that."

I sat back. "Yes, I did. Sorry."

That calmed him a little. "If it comes to this, there is one more thing you need to know."

What else could there be? But I might as well find out. "Okay."

"Whoever defeats a reaper must take their place."

"You mean...I would become the reaper?"

He nodded. "Yes."

"As in I would become the Mistress of Nightmares?"

"Exactly."

Oh, snowballs, *no*.

I wrapped up the conversation with Lucien and

went through the motions of saying goodbye to Hattie, but the truth was, a numbness had come over me. This was way more than I had bargained for. More information, more serious, and more sobering.

I didn't want to hurt anyone. And I certainly didn't want to become a reaper myself. But what was I going to do if Luna attacked Sanders? I was supposed to protect him.

Maybe she wouldn't do anything. Maybe she wouldn't even show up. But Olive had seemed so sure the woman was trouble. And Sanders had blamed her for the missing hourglass like it was a foregone conclusion.

My head hurt. And my spirits were low.

I got in the car and sat there, staring at the knob on the glove box while Greyson got behind the wheel. Today I did not want to be the Winter Princess.

I didn't want to be anything but home, in bed, with my cat curled up next to me.

Duty and responsibility could get melted.

Greyson put the key in the ignition, then let it dangle, turning to look at me instead. "You're not okay. What happened in there?"

I shook my head slowly. "I can't tell you. I promised not to. My word as winter royalty is my bond. But man, do I want to." Sharing this burden with someone would make carrying it a little easier.

If only I knew another elemental here in town that I could talk to.

He put a hand on my knee. "Jayne, there has to be a way I can help you with this. You look like you just found out someone died. And it's killing me to see you like this."

All this talk of death and murder was getting to be too much. I lifted my head. "There's nothing you can do to help. I wish there was, but there's not. Just take me home, okay? I need some time to think."

"I'm sorry. I shouldn't have brought you here."

"No, you were trying to help. And you have. I just didn't expect the end result to be this...dire."

He frowned and shook his head. I could see he was struggling, wishing he could do something. But I'd given my word to Lucien. And the last thing I needed was to upset him. Luna was just passing through, but Lucien lived here.

And so did I.

I tipped my head back as Greyson drove and closed my eyes. Was Luna really as big a problem as Olive and Sanders were making her out to be? Why would Sanders spend the evening dancing and chatting with her if he was so certain she'd want to cause him trouble?

I opened my eyes and stared at the car's ceiling. There was only one thing I could think of. It was crazy. But so was my life. And what was one more crazy thing in the midst of all this current nonsense?

Especially when that crazy thing might not be so crazy after all.

I straightened up. We were already back in town. I put my hand on Greyson's arm. "There is something you can do for me. I'm not sure you're going to like it, but you're not talking me out of it either."

"I wouldn't dream of it. Mostly because I know better. What can I do?"

"Do you know where Luna is staying?"

"No, but it can't be that hard to find out. I'm sure Birdie knows."

"Good idea. I'll call her." I got my phone out, pulled up her number and tapped the call button.

She answered right away. "Hello again, Princess. First breakfast, now a call. What a nice surprise! How are you?"

I didn't even care that she'd called me Princess and not Jayne. "I've been better, but you might be able to help with that. Do you know where Luna Nyx is staying in town?"

"Oh sure, I heard from Edna Turnbuckle yesterday. It's not every day a reaper books a room at your establishment. Which is the Black Rose, by the way. It's a lovely place, even if it is a D&B. But Edna's made a go of it. Very popular place, too. I'm sure it's down to her hospitability."

Birdie finally took a breath. Before she started talking again, I got my question in. "What's a D&B?"

"Dead and Breakfast. It's one of the places vampires stay when they come to town."

"So is Edna a vampire?"

Greyson shook his head, but said nothing.

"No," Birdie said. "She's a hobbit. They're known for their warmth and friendliness. You want to meet her? I play bridge with her twice a month. We're good friends."

"That's okay, I'll introduce myself when I get there. Thanks for the info. I owe you a stack of pancakes."

She laughed. "You don't owe me anything. I'm happy to help whenever I can."

"Thanks, Birdie." I was feeling better already. "I really appreciate it."

"You got it, Princess."

We hung up, and I looked at Greyson.

"Let me guess," he said. "You want me to take you to the Black Rose. Because I can't imagine Luna's staying anywhere else."

"I do."

"Going to see Luna is not a good idea. Not alone."

"I'm not alone." I smiled at him. "I have you."

His mouth curved. "True. Let's do this."

He turned the wheel, took us down a side street, and a couple of minutes later, we were pulling into the parking lot of a large, charming house. It wasn't as ornate as the Victorians in the neighborhood where Pandora and her boyfriend lived, but it had a real Southern appeal to it. Very welcoming.

And very popular, judging by the other cars in the lot. We parked next to a sleek black SUV.

Greyson turned off the engine and faced me. "Do you know what you're going to say?"

"I'm just going to talk to her. Get a read on her. I have to trust my gut on this."

He nodded. "That's as good a plan as any."

"I'm glad you think so, because it's all I've got." I held up a finger. "One question. Do I need to be worried about her touching me? Like with Lucien?"

"No. That's only true with him because of the glitch in his power."

"That makes me feel better."

We got out and walked to the front door. Greyson opened it and we went in. The place was quiet, but considering that it catered to vampires, and those staying here were probably asleep, that wasn't surprising.

A door at the end of the hall opened and an older woman stepped out. Mrs. Turnbuckle, I assumed. "Can I help you folks? If you're looking for a room, I'm sorry to tell you we have no vacancies. I can suggest another lovely spot just on the other side of town, however."

I smiled as pleasantly as I could considering I was about to talk to a very scary person. "Hi. My name is Jayne Frost, and this is my friend, Greyson Garrett. We don't need a room. We're here to visit a guest of yours, Luna Nyx."

The woman walked farther down the hall toward us. She had piercing brown eyes, wire-rimmed glasses, and ears with points rounder than mine. "Is she expecting you?"

"No, but she's coming by my store later today, Santa's Workshop, and I just thought I'd stop by and see her first."

Greyson stepped up so that he was at my side. "Mrs. Turnbuckle, could you ask her if she'd just give us a few minutes of her time? We won't be long."

"Why do you want to speak to me?"

We looked up. Luna stood on the second-floor landing, staring down at us. She was dressed in black, as she had been the night before, but there was something much more subdued about her today. Her dress was simpler, her hair wound into a single long braid that fell over one shoulder, and as far as I could tell, there were no spiders in it. Thankfully.

I held onto my smile. At least I think what my face was doing could be described as a smile. "I wanted to talk to you about the signing. Just for a few minutes."

"You were at the party last night."

"Yes." I leaned into Greyson a little. "We both were."

She stared at me for a long moment, her eyes narrowed. Not once did she look at Greyson, which was odd, but 'odd' was kind of losing its meaning at this point. At last, she started down the stairs.

Edna came past us and opened a set of double doors to our left. "Why don't you folks use the parlor? You won't be disturbed. Can I get you some tea? Or coffee?"

"No, we're fine." And I hoped we'd stay that way. Greyson and I went in.

Luna followed, closing the doors behind her. "What do you want?"

Her tone was smooth with almost no inflection. The lack of menace *made* it menacing. I wish I could understand how that worked, but her cool, even temperament almost made me feel like any reaction I had would be too much.

I sat. No one else was, but I didn't want to stand there and face down this tall, willowy creature on my feet. You know, just in case my knees locked up, the blood stopped flowing to my brain, and I passed out.

Greyson took the seat next to me, instantly earning boyfriend points.

Luna frowned, then also sat.

That was my cue to begin. "I appreciate you speaking to us. I wanted to come by and see you because frankly, I'm a little concerned about your visit to the store today. I think being honest with you is only fair. And there's no point in dancing around the awkwardness of this situation. So there it is."

She lifted her chin. Her eyes were so black I couldn't see where her pupils ended and irises began. For an average person, that would have been very off-putting. For a reaper who was also the Mistress of Nightmares, it was perfect. Creepy and weird, but perfect. "Why are you concerned? Why is it awkward?"

"I can give you the same answer to both of those questions. You're Tempus Sanders' ex-wife. Don't you think that's enough to make this situation a little tense?"

She shrugged and I swear something black scurried through the plaits of her braid. So much for the spiders being gone. "You saw Tempus and me together last night. How friendly we were. What are you worried about?"

"Honestly, that maybe things won't be so friendly today." I didn't want to tell her about what had happened this morning. I wasn't going to be the reason she got mad at him. "I'm the manager of the store. It's my responsibility to make sure things go smoothly, not just for Tempus as my guest, but for the customers who will be attending and for my employees who will be working. I don't want any disruptions anywhere. That's it. That's why I'm here."

She leaned forward and I definitely saw movement at her hairline. I tamped down the urge to grimace. "I understand. You're just doing your job. I commend that, actually."

"Thank you." And I meant it. I hadn't expected a compliment from her. Didn't mean we were best friends or anything, but it was a start. "So can you promise me that your visit today will be just as friendly as last night's?"

She smiled. "No."

I wasn't sure what to say to that.

She tipped her head. "That is as much up to Tempus as it is me, isn't it?"

"I suppose." Which meant I was going to have to talk to him too. Snowballs.

Then Luna waved her hand at Greyson. "Could I

speak to you alone?"

I could sense Greyson tense up, but I felt differently about Luna than I had a few minutes ago. And if I could survive being alone with Lucien, I could certainly survive Luna. "Sure." I looked at him. "Give us a sec?"

He nodded, but sent Luna a sharp glance. "I'll be in the hall."

When he left, Luna spoke again. "You are not just a winter elf, are you?"

I played dumb. Partly because I really wasn't sure what she was headed for. And partly because I wasn't going to volunteer any more personal info than I had to. "No. I'm also the Winter Princess, heir to the Winter Throne."

She laughed, a breathy sound like wind through bare branches. "That's not what I meant. You have some elemental in you, don't you?"

Oh, that. "Yes, I do. Not much, though. Not enough to give me any kind of power advantage." Best to confess that up front in case she thought she needed to show off her skills to make a point. Also, I'd rather she underestimate me. Just in case.

She sat back and smoothed her dress over her thin legs. "But enough to make us kin. In the way that all elementals are kin to one another."

I'd never felt that way, but then I was a winter elf through and through, despite my bloodlines. And really, arguing with her wasn't going to get me anywhere. I just nodded and said, "Uh-huh."

"That's why I'm going to tell you why I'm really here."

I was getting all kinds of special info today. I suppressed a groan. "Oh? Why's that?"

Her chest rose and fell with a sudden breath. "I'm here…to get Tempus back."

I blinked a few times before words came to me. I hadn't expected that. "Really?"

Her mouth bent into an expression of sadness. "I miss him. I know he can be an acquired taste, but I still love him. I thought if I came to town to see him at his book signing, he'd see that things could still be good between us. And they were last night. But now I don't know."

All of a sudden, I felt for her. And I still didn't want to tell her what had happened this morning, but it didn't seem to me that Tempus was in any rush to reunite. "Maybe the book signing isn't the best place. Maybe you should try to get some alone time with him, you know? Like after it's all said and done. Then he can concentrate on you."

She flattened her hands on her lap and stared at them. "I know you don't want me there, but I need to see him. I need him to know I support him. And I promise I won't make trouble." She lifted her head to look at me again. "Unless you try to stop me from being there."

I knew a threat when I heard one. I wasn't about to be bullied. I dropped the temperature in the room about thirty degrees to underline my words. "Miss Nyx, I won't stop you from being there." Ice vapor followed my words out of my mouth. "But I will have you escorted out if you do anything to disrupt the event."

She snorted, like she didn't believe I'd do any such thing.

"Does that amuse you?" I let the temp creep down a few more degrees. A crackling sound filled the room as fingers of frost inched across the windows. I stood up, doing my best to keep my eyes off the scythe hanging at her waist. "Because I can guarantee it won't amuse Tempus. You do anything to ruin this book signing for him and your chances of a reunion are definitely over."

Her expression sobered.

I hoped that meant I'd gotten through to her. "Thank you for your time. Now if you'll excuse me, I have a very busy day ahead of me."

I walked out without waiting for a reply, head up, shoulders straight. It was a walk I'd seen my mother do many times. But it was harder than it looked to turn my back on Luna.

I grabbed hold of Greyson's arm as I joined him in the hall. "Car," I said.

He nodded and went ahead of me, getting the door to the D&B.

We were half a block away before I exhaled. "That was not fun." I lifted my hands. They were visibly trembling. "She's a scary individual."

"Two reapers in one day." Greyson shook his head. "I wish you could take the rest of it off."

"Me, too. But work will be good. It'll give me something to focus on. And if it's anything like yesterday, it'll go by fast."

"You should try to rest for a few minutes when you get back to your apartment. Lie down, give yourself some time with your eyes closed to just mellow out. That sort of thing. You have time, right?"

"I do. In theory. I just don't know if I should."

"Jayne." He looked at me. "I can hear your pulse thumping. Give the stress a chance to leave. Promise me you'll at least try."

I rolled my eyes good-naturedly. "I'll try."

"Thank you."

A couple of minutes later, he dropped me off with a kiss. I checked in at the shop and found everything going smoothly. I stood behind the counter with Juniper. "Anything from upstairs?"

"Olive came down to ask where to get more of the chocolates that were in the apartment. I gave her the directions for Delaney's Delectables and she called a Ryde to take her there, although I did offer her use of a company bike. She came back with two big shopping bags, so I guess Sanders is soothing himself with sweets."

"Those would be the ones I'd pick to soothe myself with. Anything else?"

"Nope. It's been quiet since then. I guess they're resting up until the big event at three."

"Speaking of resting up, I'm going to head up to my apartment to decompress for an hour and then I'll be back down to do whatever needs doing."

"After the morning you had? Take two," she said.

"No way. That's too long. Too much to do. The hour will be fine." I didn't mention it was at Greyson's insistence I was having a nap at all.

She waved me off. "Kip and I have it covered if you decide you want longer." She grinned. "We work well together."

I smacked my hand lightly on the counter. "I knew it." I lowered my voice and leaned closer. "You like him. And he likes you. Have you broken it to Pete yet that he's got competition?"

"No, and I'm not going to. I do like Kip, but it's only as a friend. Besides, he's got a girlfriend in the NP." She sighed a little sadly. "He said something about her this morning."

"Huh. Well, that's a bummer. I like Pete and everything, but you and Kip seem—"

"We seem what?" Kip came out of one of the rows, a feather duster in his hand.

I spun to face him, feeling a little caught. "I was just saying what a great job you and Juniper are doing. You guys seem like you work well together and you've picked up the shop business like an old hand."

He smiled. At Juniper. "Thanks."

Sure, he might have a girlfriend, but I'd bet she wasn't going to last long. I shot Juniper a look. "Be back in a bit."

"Take as long as you need," she hollered after me.

I just shook my head and kept walking.

I love my bed. It's a big comfy nest of a thing. I also love sleep. I mean, what elf doesn't? We work hard, play hard, sleep hard. It's kind of an elf thing.

But the idea of napping, or resting, or whatever you wanted to call it while the shop was open didn't go down so easy with me. At least not on a day when there was a big event about to happen. Yes, I know I'd napped yesterday, but I'd had the party at Elenora's to deal with on top of everything else.

After today's signing, we were essentially done. Sanders would be leaving tomorrow morning so tonight had purposely been left free. It was his chance to explore the town if he so desired. And unless he requested my presence, which he hadn't, I was free.

So really, there wasn't anything to rest up for. Other than a slightly busier day at work than normal.

Sure, my morning had been hectic, but was that really enough to warrant a nap?

Apparently it was, because here I lay on my bed, staring up at the ceiling with a happy little black cat licking his foot next to me.

I wasn't going to actually sleep. I could feel that much. I was too restless. Then what was I doing here? Certainly not decompressing the way Greyson had hoped, because all I could think about was Luna's impending visit.

And the fact that she'd threatened me.

I rested my arm across my eyes, blocking out the light. I couldn't take the threat lightly, but then again, I couldn't exactly do anything about it until she acted on it. And then what? I grabbed for her scythe and did my best ninja moves on her?

I'd been trained to fight with the magic I had. Ice, cold, snow. I could create all kinds of weapons and defenses and distractions with the stuff. But none of that would work against a reaper. Freezing her solid was a temporary measure at best. Nothing would really defeat a reaper but their own blade, according to Lucien.

And the real kicker was I couldn't tell anyone. It would have been so nice to turn Lucien's info over to Greyson and let him handle it. After all, Luna couldn't hurt him. He was already dead. For her purposes, anyway.

I moved my arm, squinting at the light to look at Spider. He was cleaning his ear now, licking his paw and rubbing it over his head. So cute. "I have to keep my word, don't I?"

He stopped to look at me. "What's word?"

"It's the same as a promise. I told someone I would do something. I gave them my word I would do what I said." And I'd just answered my own question.

He stood, suddenly excited. "Like feed Spider?"

"Silly cat, I fed you ten minutes ago when I came in. And that's more than my word, that's a given. Now lay down and take a nap."

He turned his head this way and that as if he couldn't quite understand why he wasn't getting more food. "Spider likes Chicken Party."

"I know. But it's nap time, not Chicken Party time."

He curled up next to me, heaving out a big sigh.

I grinned and went back to staring at the ceiling.

Then I must have taken my own advice, because the next thing I knew I was back in the store, but it wasn't exactly the store. It was a dark, swampy version of it. A dream version. And in that dream the store was now outside and it was night. Drifting clouds gave an occasional glimpse of a crescent moon.

Clumps of Spanish moss hung from the rows of toys. In the distance an owl hooted. I walked through the aisles and mud sucked at my feet. I glanced down. I was definitely outside. What the snow was going on?

"Juniper? Buttercup? Pete?" Pete didn't work here. Why was I calling for him?

A grunting noise came from behind me. I turned around to see Juniper standing there. Except she wasn't the Juniper I knew and loved, but zombie Juniper. Her teeth were all rotten and black and her eyes were sunken in like she'd already begun decomposing.

I jerked back, horrified, and a shriek ripped from my throat. Hands clutched at me from behind. I spun to see Kip reaching for me. His lower jaw hung loose off his face. He was a zombie too.

I screamed as he grabbed me again. For a dead guy, he was surprisingly strong. He was shaking me, pulling at me. I tried to shove him away, tried to—

"Jayne, wake up."

I blinked, sucked in a big gulp of air and stared up at Buttercup. My heart pounded. Was she a zombie? No. I was awake.

Tell that to my thumping pulse.

"You okay?" She sat on the side of my bed, looking very concerned. "I heard you scream from across the hall. Good thing you gave me a spare key. I thought you were getting murdered in here."

I sat up, my breath still coming in deep swallows, but I wasn't scared anymore. I was angry. I knew exactly what had just happened. And what had been happening. "That woman did this on purpose. She's *been* doing it."

Buttercup shook her head. "I have no idea what you're talking about. You sure you're okay?"

"I'm fine." I gave her the rundown about Luna, my visit to her and what her powers were.

Buttercup's brows shot up. "Mistress of Nightmares, huh? She's definitely got your number then."

I nodded. "And she's done it three times now."

"Wow."

"Exactly. Enough is enough."

Buttercup got off the bed and stood beside it. "What are you going to do?"

"I have an idea." I pushed to my feet. I was charged up and ready to act. If Luna showed up now,

I'd have no problem going for her scythe. Still not sure I could use it, but I'd at least get my hands on it. Maybe that would be enough to get her to behave.

"You need me to do anything? Help in any way?"

"Nope. I know exactly what I need to do and I can handle it on my own."

I biked to Ever After in record time. I'd texted Corette before I'd left, but had yet to get a response. I hoped that didn't mean this was a lost cause. I left the bike at the curb and walked into the shop. There was something soothing about that sea of white dresses. Reminded me of the snow drifts back home. I looked around for Corette, hoping I wasn't disturbing her.

I didn't have to look long.

She walked toward me, phone in hand. "I just got your message. Come on back to my office."

"Thanks." We walked together, her in a pretty navy suit and pearls, me in a Howler's T-shirt and yoga pants. I probably could have changed, but time had been of the essence. "I appreciate you giving me a few minutes."

"You caught me at the right moment." We went into her office and she closed the door. "I have an hour between appointments. But your text didn't say much."

It hadn't. All I'd sent was *Urgently need your help*.

She gestured for me to sit as she took the chair behind her desk. "What can I do for you?"

"I'm being targeted by someone very powerful. And I need your help to keep them out of my head."

Her eyes widened slightly. "I'm going to need a few more details."

I told her everything I could. About Luna, about the nightmares, about her desire to get Sanders back. The info about the scythe and elementals I held onto since it wasn't mine to share. "What do you think? Can you help?"

She didn't exactly smile, but there was a determined light in her eyes. "Preventing nightmares is an easy enough thing, but this is more than that. It's going to take more than a simple spell."

"That sounds complicated."

"Maybe for ordinary witches, but not for the Williams women." She lifted a finger. "Let me make a few calls…"

Less than half an hour later, I stood in Pandora Williams' spell room. It was in the well-stocked attic of her boyfriend's house, a gorgeous restored Victorian that I'd visited very briefly a few months ago. I'd been worried about getting arrested then.

Now I was worried that I might lose my life. But Pandora had cast a spell of protection on me then, so I imagined that whatever spell she, her sister Marigold, and their mother Corette were about to create would be three times as effective.

I hoped so. I didn't have a lot of other options.

The three women stood only a few steps away from me, but their attention was on each other and preparations for the spellcasting. It was pretty interesting. Cold magic I knew backwards and forwards, but witchcraft was completely foreign. Everything about this space—the jars, bottles, and boxes filling the shelves that lined the walls, the table of tools and implements the women were gathered around, and the curiously-titled books stacked in neat piles here and there—seemed as alien to me as Cooper's heat magic.

I was content to just stand there and listen while they prepared. I figured maybe I'd learn something.

Marigold unpacked the bag she'd brought, laying smaller packets on the table where Pandora had set out a mortar and pestle. "Chamomile, sage, and lavender. And vervain for the sachets." She glanced over and smiled at me. "All organically grown and from my garden."

I nodded. "Nice."

Corette took glass jars off the shelves and brought the containers to the table. "Ashes, sand, and salt."

Pandora carried a carved wooden box over from the other side of the attic. "Silver dust." She put the box down, then pulled a long, black feather from the pocket of her apron. "And a raven's feather."

"Cole's?" Marigold asked.

I had no idea why the feather could be Pandora's boyfriend's, but I wasn't going to question it. Maybe he was a witch too.

"No," she said. "This isn't from a familiar."

More stuff I didn't understand.

Corette drew a slim, silver blade from a burgundy leather sheath and turned toward me. "For this spell to be as effective as we can make it, a few drops of your blood will be required. I promise we'll only take what's required for the spell. Nothing more."

Her tone was almost apologetic and I could sense her reluctance to ask me. Almost like she expected me to refuse. I guess blood was a pretty powerful thing. But they were doing me a favor. A huge one. I wasn't going to question their intent. I smiled and stuck my hand out. "Whatever you need."

"Thank you." She took my hand and drew me closer to the mortar, holding my hand over it as she pricked my finger.

I flinched, then laughed. "I'm kind of a big baby when it comes to pain."

"We all are." She squeezed a few drops into the bowl. "That's it. All done."

I pressed my thumb against my forefinger. It throbbed a little. "What do you need me to do now?"

"Nothing yet," Pandora said. "We have to mix the rest first."

"Okay." I stepped out of their way and watched. "I know I'm not a witch and this is probably secret stuff, but if you can tell me what you're doing, I'd love to know."

Pandora smiled. "Sure, we can share some of it with you." She held up a glass jar. "This is sand collected under a full moon. It represents the dream world." She measured some into the mortar.

Marigold held up the packets she'd brought. "And these plants—chamomile, lavender, and sage—are for calming and protection." She emptied them into the mortar as well. "The vervain will remain whole and a sprig will go into each of the little bags we're going to prepare."

Corette held up another glass jar. "These are ashes collected from burned white oak. They represent death."

"The reaper," I whispered.

She nodded and tipped some into the mix. "Yes."

Then she picked up a new jar. "And this is salt. It represents life."

"Me?"

"In a way, yes. But it is also the thing we wish to preserve." She sprinkled a handful of the white crystals over the ashes. "The blood is what ties this magic to you."

Pandora added a pinch of the silver dust. "The silver is the spirit world." Then she lifted the feather. "And this feather is the natural world. The one we walk in." She stirred it through the ingredients in the bowl. "It binds all these things together." She put the feather down and passed the mortar to Marigold.

She picked up the pestle and ground it into the mix as she spoke a few words over and over. "Peace and rest, light and peace, may all nightmares from this point cease."

I was riveted. It was like being admitted to a secret club. Sure, I'd never really be a member, but getting to watch all this was pretty cool.

"What now?" I asked when she stopped chanting.

"Now you stand in the center of the room," a voice said behind me.

I turned around to see a petite woman with shellacked salmon hair that matched her pantsuit. She was as sheer as a set of curtains and hovering three feet off the ground. I sucked in a breath. "You're not all there."

Corette rushed to my side. "No, she's not, but she won't hurt you."

"Gertrude," Pandora admonished. "You promised not to make an appearance."

135

So this was Gertrude. Two ghosts and two reapers in one day. Or as it was otherwise known, life in Nocturne Falls.

Gertrude pouted. "I said I wouldn't interrupt the spell. And I haven't."

I pointed. Maybe not the most polite thing to do, but I was a little stunned. "She's a ghost." I meant it as a question, but I already knew the answer. Two in one day. That seriously had to be a record, even for Nocturne Falls.

"Yes, she is and I'm sorry." Corette took hold of my arm with the sort of firmness that suggested she thought I might need propping up. "Gertrude, I know we're in your space, but Jayne isn't used to such appearances. And she has enough to deal with."

"Oh?" Gertrude's eyes widened happily. "What else has happened?"

I shook my head. "I don't know where to start."

Corette patted my arm. "You don't need to." She addressed the ghost again. "Gertrude, we're just about to finish this spell. If you would be so kind…"

Gertrude hovered a little higher. "I could help."

"You can?" Maybe I shouldn't have asked, but there was something so sincere about the little old lady ghost I couldn't help myself.

"Sure, honey. I've been doing spells since before the lot of you were born." She did a little twirl, arms outstretched. "Whose spell-room do you think you're standing in?"

I glanced at Pandora.

She shrugged. "This was her house."

I looked at Gertrude again, only to find she was

floating mere inches away from me. I startled. The day was really starting to get to me and there was a lot of it left to get through. I took a breath before I spoke. "I'm happy to have extra help. Anything to keep Luna from being able to affect me."

"Who's Luna?" Gertrude asked.

I explained as briefly as I could. "So you see why I need the spell to keep the nightmares away."

"Oh, yes." Gertrude straightened. As much as an apparition could. Then she clapped her hands, which somehow made noise. "Form a circle, ladies. Let's charge this spell." She waved a hand at me. "You, into the center."

I moved as she directed, then Pandora handed me the bowl with all the ingredients in it. "Hang on to that."

I nodded as she joined Marigold, Corette and Gertrude in a loose circle around me. They held their hands out, palms up, and chanted the same words Marigold had said before. Three times they repeated the phrases, then finished with, "So mote it be."

Gertrude was the first to break formation. She snapped her fingers at Pandora. "You have the muslin?"

"I do." Pandora took the bowl from me. "We're going to divide this into bags for you."

Marigold held up three teabag-sized muslin pouches. "One you'll wear around your neck, one to put under your pillow, and one to put in your store." She smiled. "Not that you ever sleep there, but it'll give you a little added protection against the reaper."

"That's great, thank you." While the women

worked, I glanced at Gertrude. "Do you like other ghosts? Because I know someone who could use some company."

She sighed. "I can't seem to leave this attic."

"Bummer."

"Indeed."

Corette walked over, three pouches in her hand, one hung on a long white ribbon. "Here you are. Put that one on and don't take it off."

"Thank you." I took them from her, slipping the ribbon around my neck and tucking the pouch under my T-shirt. It actually smelled pretty nice. "Anything else I need to know?"

"Just be careful, Princess."

"I will. And I really appreciate this."

Corette smiled. "We're happy to help."

"I hate to get spelled and run, but I should return to the store." I needed to put decent clothes on and get myself ready for the signing.

"You want a lift?" Marigold asked. "I'm going back to the florist shop. I can drop you off. I just need to help Pandy clean up."

"That would be great, but I need to go back to your mom's store. I rode one of the company bikes there."

Marigold laughed. "I drive a big old SUV. I can swing by there and we'll throw it in the back."

"If you don't mind, that would be nice. Thank you."

Corette made shooing motions at us. "You girls go on. Pandora and I will put everything away."

"Thanks, Mom." Marigold headed down the stairs

and I followed her right out of the house.

She drove a black SUV that kind of reminded me of what the Ryde drivers favored, except those vehicles were always pristine inside. This one had granola bar wrappers on the floor along with a pair of pink sneakers and a jump rope. A white sweatshirt jacket decorated with a sequined kitten applique lay across one of the rear passenger seats.

She saw me looking and laughed as she pulled out of Pandora's driveway. "I have a daughter. Saffron. She's nine. And not the neatest."

I couldn't imagine having another person dependent on me. Taking care of Spider was probably a good start, though nothing like having a kid. "Is she a witch too? Sorry if that's a dumb question. I don't know how that works."

"Not a dumb question. And yes, she is, but we don't really get our powers until about age thirteen." Marigold smiled. "Right now, Saffie's main concerns are Mini Molly dolls, Tiny Pets, and Charlie Merrow."

"Hey, we sell those at the store. Well, not Charlie. You know what I mean."

Marigold laughed. "I do. She earns a new accessory each week if she does all the chores on her chart. I'll have to bring her in."

"Let me know before you come so I can make sure you get the friends and family discount." By which I meant free. After the help she and her family had given me, there was no way I'd let her pay for a few toys.

"Very kind of you."

"Well, I appreciate all you guys have done for

me." She stopped in front of her mom's shop and I opened the door to hop out and grab the bike. "Including the ride home."

"No problem." She got out to help me and we were back on our way in two minutes.

A few minutes after that, she pulled up to the warehouse curb and threw the gearshift into Park. We got the bike unloaded and I thanked her again. "I really do appreciate this. All of it."

She nodded. "You're welcome. And have a great day."

"I will now."

She drove off. I went inside, put the bike on the rack, then went straight to my apartment, where I tucked the second muslin bag under my pillow.

Luna would not be bothering me again.

The second and final signing was twenty minutes away and everything was as ready as it could be. I was in my second super-professional-manager outfit: a pale gray sheath dress with a slim black belt and less sensible but killer black heels. Pearls and diamond studs to accessorize, of course. The shoes kept it from being boring. Really it was corporate sexy. There was power in feeling this pulled together. Along with the magic pouch around my neck, it gave me a confidence boost. Exactly what I might need if Luna showed up.

Everything else was just as on point. The display table was stocked with books (which were already being snatched up by customers in record numbers). The signing area was neat and tidy, awaiting Sanders' arrival. And everyone was in their place. Juniper was on the register, Holly was ready to check receipts in the signing line and Rowley was working the floor while Kip handled restocking.

But most importantly, the third muslin bag was tucked under the cash drawer of the register. The register seemed like the heart of the shop, so that's where I'd put the pouch.

That didn't mean I wasn't sweating a little bit, though. Sure, I had the witches' magic, and I didn't doubt the protection they'd given me against nightmares would work, but there was still most likely a reaper headed to my store.

A reaper. The more those words repeated in my head, the more I could feel myself getting spun up.

I checked my watch. Fifteen minutes. Sanders would be down shortly, but I could spare a moment. I hustled to my office and dug into the stash of eggnog fudge that had arrived from my aunt Martha with the last shipment of books.

She'd worked out a deal with Delaney Ellingham to sell the fudge in Delaney's shop, but my aunt, being my aunt, always made sure each shipment that came through included a small box for me. And sometimes, more often than that.

It was good to be this loved.

I leaned back in my chair and took a bite. The sweet, creamy, sugary explosion of flavor made my teeth ache and my happy endorphins kick in. I popped the rest into my mouth and relaxed even more, closing my eyes and enjoying a moment of pure peace. I could do this. Luna wasn't going to be a problem. I just had to keep telling myself that.

"Knock, knock."

I opened my eyes at the familiar voice. "Hey Co-op."

"Hi, Jay." He leaned against the door frame, hands in his pockets.

"What brings you by?" He was in his uniform, which added extra degrees to his already off-the-charts hotness. All in all, a very nice distraction that was slightly sweeter than the fudge I'd just eaten.

"You." He smiled. "Just wanted to see how you were doing."

Wasn't that nice? "Crazy." I shrugged. "But what's new? I'll be fine. I can handle this." That last bit was more for me than him.

"You look great, but..." He glanced at his watch. "Doesn't the signing start in a few minutes?"

I checked the time. Ten minutes. "Yes. Snowballs. Sanders isn't standing out in the warehouse looking for me, is he?"

Cooper checked over his shoulder. "Nope. Just me."

I jumped to my feet. "He'd better be on his way down here, because if something else is going on—"

The elevator's chime interrupted me and I heard the doors slide open. "Please tell me that's him."

Cooper took a second look and nodded. "Yep. I'll let you get to work. You want to hang out later? I could bring dinner. There's a new BBQ place in town that's supposed to do killer ribs, Big Daddy Bones. Have you tried them yet?"

"Nope, but I'm in." I shut my desk drawer and headed for the door, even though Cooper was still blocking it. "Seven?"

"Sounds good. See you then. And I'll let myself out so you can deal with Sanders." He moved so I could pass, but as I slid by, he nuzzled my neck and inhaled, whispering, "You smell nice."

I didn't have time to tell him it was the juju bag tucked beneath my dress, but I was suddenly very glad the spell hadn't required anything funky like tail of newt or dried bat liver. "Thanks." I squeezed his bicep. More for me than for him. "See you for dinner."

He grinned and I made my way to Sanders, who was standing by the shop door now. Olive was at his side, checking something off on her pad. Her messenger bag was slung across her body, as full as it had been the first time. I imagined it contained all the same supplies.

I stopped in front of them as Cooper exited the building. "I trust the rest of your day has been uneventful?"

"Ah, yes," Sanders said. He'd changed into sea green fancy pajamas, his hourglass safely at his side on its cord. "I had a most refreshing nap after breakfast."

Olive didn't look up from her work, just grunted something that I guessed was a sound of agreement.

"Great. All ready for the last signing?" I rubbed my hands together. "The shop is busy."

He narrowed his eyes. "Will the same number of people show up, do you think?"

"We're definitely hoping that's the case, and judging by the look of things, it should be close." I certainly hoped we were busy, because we had a mountain of books on hand. And being busy made the time fly. Not to mention, I still wanted to impress my father and uncle with some exceptional numbers. "Why don't we go in and get things started?"

He nodded. "Lead the way."

I got him and Olive situated in the signing area, then headed to the front to see how the crowd (which had definitely showed up) was doing. I almost ran into Greyson as I rounded the last row. "Hi."

He smiled. "Hi yourself. You look lovely. How's it going?"

"Thanks." He didn't look bad either, but then he never did. "Just getting started."

"No sign of our special guest then?"

"Not yet."

His nostrils flared. "You've taken some precautions, I see."

"You can smell that?"

"Vervain. Also salt, ash, lavender." His nose wrinkled. "And silver. I know what the Romani would use that combination for. Who made it for you?"

The man was wise about so many things. I liked that. Handsome and smart was a great combo. "The witches fixed me up. Corette and two of her daughters."

"Good. That's very good."

"Glad you approve."

"I should have thought of it myself." He stepped to the side. "I know you're busy and I don't want to be in the way so just tell me where to stand."

With Holly already working the signing line, the best place for Greyson was behind the register. It was the easiest spot for him to watch the customers coming in without being too conspicuous. Juniper wasn't crazy about vampires, but I was hoping she'd be all right with this temporary situation. Fingers crossed, anyway. I gave Greyson a little nudge with my hip. "Follow me."

I led him through the crowd. Juniper was occupied with a customer buying a book, but I went behind the counter and pulled her aside as soon as she handed him his purchase. "I'd really like Greyson to stand back here with you today. He's agreed to act as additional security in case Luna shows up. That's it. You cool with that?"

Juniper stared at Greyson on the other side of the counter, giving him a quick appraisal. "You eat today?"

"I did," Greyson answered.

Juniper nodded. "Fine with me."

"Thank you." I looked at Greyson, then tipped my head toward the spot next to me.

He joined me behind the counter. "You want me to pitch in? Put stuff in sacks, that sort of thing?"

I must have given him an odd expression.

"What?" He smiled. "You don't think I can work retail?"

"I'm sure you can. I just can't quite picture it. Especially in your VOD attire." Which today was a slight deviation from the standard Vampire On Duty look for him—black leather pants with a simple black tee and a black canvas moto jacket. I realized he'd dressed down a little. Most likely for me. "But if you want to help, I don't think Juniper would say no."

"No, I wouldn't," Juniper agreed. "At least until it slows down."

"You got it," Greyson answered.

"But don't lose track of what you're here for," I told Greyson.

"No chance of that. She won't get by unnoticed."

I stepped out from behind the counter, my back to the door. "I'll leave you to it then, and go see how things are going with Sanders."

Greyson's gaze went past me. "Or not."

I turned.

Luna stood behind me.

I sucked in a breath. Son of a nutcracker. Why had she come at the start of the signing? I had a line of people waiting to see Sanders, and another line on the sidewalk outside the shop. I'd really thought she would have come toward the end, when things had died down.

No pun intended.

I pasted a smile on my face and approached her. She was dressed how I'd always seen her, all in black. Spiders and everything. Except today she also had black baby's breath in her hair, worn like a crown. "Luna. You came."

She smiled right back at me, but it was a cold expression. "I said I would. And here I am." She glanced past me, maybe looking for Sanders. "How does this work? As you can imagine, I've never been to a book signing before."

I nodded. "It's easy. You buy a book, then take the book and your receipt with you while you wait in this line." I gestured to the line snaking through the store. "One of the employees will check your receipt and mark it for you, then when you get to the front, Tempus will sign your book. I'm sure he'll be thrilled to see you."

I wasn't sure about that at all. I'd have to give him

a heads-up as soon as I got Luna situated. And because the line was already so long, it would take at least half an hour, maybe forty-five minutes for her to see Sanders. That was a long time for her to be in my store.

Too long.

I tried to think about what my dad would do in a situation like this. How he would handle someone he wanted to spend as little time with as possible. Kill them with kindness, my father was fond of saying.

My father was a smart man.

I picked a book off the table. If getting rid of her early cost me a book, that was a small price to pay. "But I know you must be eager to see him, so take this book on the house and stand here by the register for a moment." Where Greyson could watch her. "I want to tell Sanders it's okay to start the signing, and then I'll be right back."

She took the book from me, her smile faltering as we drew closer together. Her nose twitched. Was she picking up on the magic the witches had created for me? If so, I hoped she understood that I was wise to her games—and maybe even figured out that I wasn't just anyone to be fooled with. I was the Winter Princess, after all. For whatever that was worth.

"Something wrong?" I asked.

Her eyes narrowed, but she shook her head. "No." Then her smile returned, thin, but there. "I'll wait right here."

"Be right back." I wanted to look at Greyson, but I didn't want to draw her attention to him, so I walked away without any contact. I swear I could sense him watching Luna, though.

Sanders had already started signing books when I rounded the corner. He liked to talk to everyone, really give them their money's worth. It was fantastic, really, and probably why we had such a big crowd on day two. There were definitely repeat customers in the mix.

But it meant that things moved slowly and I needed Luna out as soon as possible. The longer she was here, the more chance there was for something to go wrong. And I did not need a lethal mistake in my shop.

I sidled up to Olive. "I need to get a special customer in ahead of the line."

She frowned at me. "Who?"

"You know who."

"Tall, dark, and skeletal?"

"That's the one."

Olive sighed. "Bring her back."

"I need to tell Sanders she's here."

"I'll prep him." She cut her eyes in his direction. He was gabbing away with a grandmother getting three copies signed. "He'll probably be thrilled."

"Even after this morning? He was so quick to blame her."

She made a face. "Yes, even after that. Before he took his nap, he was actually talking about how he owed her an apology." She sighed. "What is it with men? It's like he's blinded by feminine wiles and sexual charms or something."

I didn't particularly think Luna was all that sexy, but what did I know about Sanders' taste in women?

"They say there's a lid for every pot, right?"

Her eyes stayed on him, but her gaze took on a dark glint. "I suppose."

"I'll just go get her."

Olive nodded, but never took her eyes off him. Was she worried about her boss? I didn't blame her, because I was too.

If the Sandman was still in love with the Mistress of Nightmares, we might all be in trouble.

Sanders wasn't just happy that Luna had shown up, he was ecstatic. With an enormous grin on his face, he jumped out of his chair, knocking it over. "Luna!"

Olive righted it, her expression fixed into a solemn but otherwise blank mask.

"You came!" He came around the signing table and took Luna's hands in his as I stepped out of the way. "I'm so glad you did."

"I said I would." She smiled the warmest smile I'd seen on her so far today. It was the same way she'd looked at him last night. "I'm so very proud of you, Tempus. Your own book. It's very exciting."

I retreated to the edge of the room and glanced at the people in line, waiting for someone to be cranky about Luna's massive line jump, but they all seemed enthralled by the scene unfolding before them. I understood. Tempus and Luna made a pretty interesting couple. Of course, the possibility existed that Luna might be using some kind of magic to influence them, but I didn't really know if that was in her skill set or not.

"How's it going?" Greyson appeared at my side. His cinnamon-spice scent wafted over the herby smell of the pouch tucked beneath my dress.

"Good." I leaned into him a little so that I could keep my voice down. "They seem genuinely glad to be in each other's company."

"They do. Are they getting back together?"

"Not sure. But they can figure that out on their own time. Right now, I need him to sign her book so she can leave and we can get back to business."

I felt him move slightly. "The crowd seems okay with it."

My gaze stayed on Tempus and Luna. "For now. Let them wait five more minutes and this little reunion won't be nearly so cute."

"You want me to escort her out if it goes too long?"

"Not until I've given it my best diplomatic effort, but if she resists, you can have at it."

Luna had the book I'd given her tucked under her arm. She presented it to Sanders. "I would be honored if you would sign this for me."

I relaxed a little. Maybe this wasn't going to take as long as I thought.

Sanders' smile grew impossibly larger. "The honor would be mine. But only if you'll have dinner with me this evening."

She laughed—a sound that was flat out astonishing coming from her—and nodded. "That would be wonderful. But where will we go?"

"Don't give it another thought. My assistant will take care of it." Sanders took the book from Luna and sat to sign it.

Olive's only reaction to his announcement was to reach for her phone and start tapping away. Presumably she was looking up suitable local restaurants. If she ever quit working for him, I would hire her. She might not be the cheeriest of people, but the woman had mad organizational skills. I could use someone that willing and efficient. I'd have to tell my dad.

Sanders finished whatever he was writing in Luna's book with a swooping flourish and handed the book back to her. Then he stood, took Luna's hand, and presented her to the crowd as he spoke to them. "Thank you all for your patience so that I might sign a book for my…" He glanced at her, his eyes soft and dreamy. The guy had it bad. He kissed her hand. "My wife, the lovely Luna Nyx."

Wife?

The crowd cheered and gasped and clapped. I started to make a face, then stopped myself before anyone saw me. Clearly, Sanders wasn't the only one buying what Luna was selling. The customers in the store were eating this up.

I leaned toward Greyson. "If the crowd is responding to her like that, there's no way they're seeing her in the same form we are, right? All those spiders and the Goth creepiness would have to freak some of them out."

"Right," he answered. "They don't see any of that, just like they don't see my fangs or your pointed ears. That's the beauty of this town and the bespelled water—it blurs all that away."

That amazing magic was what made it possible for Nocturne Falls to be a supernatural safe haven. That part I knew. "So what do they see?"

"My guess is they see a Morticia Addams type. A tall, striking woman who favors the darker side of life. Much like Sanders most likely resembles a self-help guru who touts the benefits of meditation and low-impact yoga."

"Huh. I never thought about how they saw him. Interesting." And it explained why they weren't as weirded out by Luna as the rest of us were.

Sanders cleared his throat in an attempt to get the crowd's attention. It worked. "Now, if you'll just excuse me for a few minutes while I escort Luna out, when I return I will be all yours."

There were a few groans from the crowd, confirming my thoughts that they were only going to put up with this interruption for so long.

I stepped forward, smiling brightly. This wasn't just about keeping the crowd happy. I wasn't about to let her get him alone. Not yet, anyway. Not while he was still on company time. The last thing I needed was Sanders disappearing in the middle of the signing for a make-out session. Which, *ew*. "I'll see her out, Mr. Sanders. I know Luna understands how busy you are." I looked at her. "I'm sure you don't want to pull him away from his fans, do you?"

Her gaze went cold and her smile lost its warmth. "No, of course not." She turned to Sanders, and kissed him on the cheek as she patted his chest. "Stay, my darling. I will see you tonight."

Olive caught my eye and gave me the tiniest grin, like she understood what I'd done and approved. Something about that vote of confidence boosted my spirts further.

"Very kind of you, Jayne." Sanders nodded at me.

I gave him a little bow. "I'll take good care of her, Mr. Sanders."

"Well, well," Greyson whispered. "Nicely done, Princess."

I caught his eye and gave him a look to let him know I'd heard, then I turned my attention to Luna. "Right this way, Ms. Nyx."

I started forward, doing my best to part the crowd. I looked back once to make sure she was following me. She was. Glaring daggers at me, too. Whatever. Dirty looks weren't going to do me any harm.

I stopped at the door, keeping my smile tacked on. Greyson was already back behind the register. "Thank you for joining us, Luna. I'm sure you and Tempus will have a lovely evening. I wish you both all the best."

I waited for her to leave. She didn't.

She held up the book. "I still need to pay for this."

"Oh no, that's on the house. My gift to you." A stream of customers eddied around us. I stayed put, hoping she'd get the drift and flow on out the door with them.

"Trying to get rid of me, hmm?"

I shook my head more vigorously than I meant to. "Not at all. You're welcome to stay and look around as long as you like. All our customers are. But it's a busy day, as you can see, and my main focus is the signing and making sure the day goes as smoothly as possible for Tempus' sake. If there's something else you need, I'll be happy to have one of my employees help you."

Her eyes narrowed and she glided closer to me. "I know you want me gone. I know you don't like me. That you fear me. Why else would you wear such magic around you?"

"Magic?" Yes, I was playing dumb. But what was I going to do? Admit I'd had some witchy help?

Her fingers circled in the air in the front of me, her black, pointed fingernails gleaming in the bright shop lights. "I can smell it on you."

This whole business was wearing me out. Playing dumb had been...dumb. And my cheeks hurt from fake smiling. So I stopped. "I'm not afraid of you, Luna. Nor am I your biggest fan, but if you wanted me to like you, maybe you should have approached things differently."

"I don't know what you mean."

Now who was playing dumb? "And I don't appreciate the nightmares that show up every time I close my eyes."

Her mouth opened slightly like she was surprised. "What?"

I rolled my eyes. Maybe not the best response, but come on. "They started the night Sanders arrived. The same night you checked into the Black Rose." I'd gotten that info from Birdie. "I really don't understand why you singled me out, but if you think I'm some kind of competition for Sanders, you're wrong. Ice cold wrong."

"Competition? I…" She shook her head. "I've done no such thing."

Oh good, we were done telling the truth. "So those nightmares were just a coincidence? Yeah, I'm sure. Look, you paid your visit and showed your support and you got what you wanted, right? You and Tempus on the road to reunion. If there's nothing else, I need to get back to work."

She hesitated. "I didn't create those nightmares. I swear I didn't."

She could swear all she wanted to, but the fact remained that she *was* the Mistress of Nightmares.

Greyson was suddenly next to me. "Perhaps I can be of assistance?"

Luna's gaze shifted to him. "No, thank you. I was just leaving." Her expression was curious and unreadable for a moment, then turned resigned as she looked at me. "Thank you for the book."

The woman was a puzzle. "You're welcome."

"I'd be happy to escort you, Ms. Nyx. Right this way," Greyson said. He led her out of the shop.

The door closed behind them and I exhaled. I was trembling a little. Standing up to a reaper was taxing. I took a few deep breaths. Chocolate would help, but I didn't have time for that. The shop was packed.

I just couldn't figure out why she'd lied about the nightmares. Had she really thought I'd be interested in Sanders? Was my elemental bloodline enough to make me a threat? It didn't matter. It was over now. I touched the little pouch through the fabric of my dress. Tonight, I would sleep easy.

No matter what the Mistress of Nightmares did or didn't do.

Another signing, another success. We'd exceeded our numbers from the day before. The register tape in front of me proved it. I chalked up the record sales to word of mouth. Not only did *Hush, Little Baby* send kids off to dreamland as quickly as it promised, but Sanders was a show all on his own. Customers had come out in droves, buying books to give away just as an excuse to see him.

I'd heard numerous people in line talking about how he'd wished them pleasant dreams the day before and how their dreams that night had been more amazing than any they'd ever had.

Meanwhile, I'd had Spider as a genuine, giant arachnid and zombie friends.

I put my pencil down, leaned back in my office chair, and popped another piece of eggnog fudge. I knew Cooper was coming over in an hour and a half with ribs, but there was always room for sugar. And I'd earned it today.

I kicked my feet up and grabbed my phone to send

a quick text to Greyson. *Thanks again.*

He'd walked Luna all the way back to the Black Rose, which was definitely above and beyond what I'd expected. I owed him. Maybe I'd take him out. Dinner at Café Claude. We hadn't been in a while and I loved that place.

You're welcome, came his response. *What are you doing tonight?*

Cooper's bringing me dinner.

Very nice of him.

What are you doing?

An errand for Lucien.

There was no point in asking what that errand was, so I didn't. I was tired of talking about reapers anyway. *You want to go to Café Claude this week? My treat.*

Oui.

I grinned and sent him a laughing emoji and the word *Later*. Then I tossed my phone in my bag and went upstairs.

Spider ran to me as soon as I walked into the apartment. Thankfully, I got my heels off before he started doing figure-eights through my legs, nearly tripping me. "Hungry, Mama. Big hungry."

I put my purse down, then picked him up to nuzzle him. "Poor baby. How did you survive while I was gone? Let's go check your food bowl."

As I suspected, the wet food bowl was empty and the bottom of the dry food bowl was visible. My boy was an eater.

I talked to him as I got his dinner ready. "Cooper's coming over."

Spider sat in front of his placemat and the velvet cat-Elvis painting and waited as patiently as he could. "Vampire man?"

"No, not the vampire man. Cooper's the other man. The elf." I tucked my hair behind my ear so Spider could see it. "You know who he is. He has pointed ears like mine."

Spider tipped his head like he was seeing me for the first time. "Mama is kitty?"

"No, not a kitty. An elf." I crouched to put his dishes down. "Mama is an elf and Cooper is an elf."

But Spider was already eating and that was the end of that conversation. I gave his head a little scratch and went to the bedroom to change. Yoga pants were calling my name.

Cooper showed up at six fifty-five, which was almost late for him. He held up a large brown-paper shopping bag. The mouthwatering aroma of barbeque wafted toward me. Smoke and spice and vinegar. My stomach growled.

"I take it you're ready to eat."

I grinned at him. Right now I wasn't sure what was more attractive, him or the food. "Hungry. Big hungry."

His brow wrinkled. "What?"

"Nothing. Come on in."

He set the bag on the kitchen table and pulled container after container out of it. I went to get plates and silverware.

"So?" he said. "How did the signing go? Did Luna show up?"

"Yes, but it wasn't too bad." I took a Dr Pepper out

of the fridge for me and a beer for Cooper. I had started keeping a six-pack on hand for when he stopped by. Which was considerably easier than having blood around for Greyson. Because no. "We had a few words as she was leaving, but it's over now so it's fine."

"Words? Like what?"

I handed him the beer. "She said I was afraid of her and didn't like her, and I told her if she wanted me to like her, she should have thought about that before filling my head with her nightmares. I didn't mention the one you had, because that might have been just a random nightmare. But mine have been too frequent."

"Agreed, and good for you." He clinked his beer against my Dr Pepper. "What did she say to that?"

I took a drink before answering. "She claimed she didn't have anything to do with those nightmares."

He snorted. "Sure."

"That's what I said. Anyway, Greyson walked her back to the Black Rose, where she's staying, and by now I suspect she's out to dinner with Tempus and you know what? Neither one of them is my problem anymore. So let's eat."

He leaned in and kissed me. "Good idea."

We sat down and Cooper gave me the barbeque tour. There was brisket, pulled pork, and lots of ribs, plus coleslaw, baked beans, green beans with ham, cornbread, and pickles.

I served myself a little of everything. "You did good, fireman."

"Thanks." He heaped food onto his own plate,

looking very pleased with himself.

I stabbed a bite of pulled pork and lifted my fork to him. "Cheers."

"Cheers," he answered.

Then everything went black.

I straightened with a groan. I felt like I'd been hit on the head. Not because my head hurt, but because everything felt off. I was groggy, like I'd just woken up. "What the snowballs just happened?"

"Did we..." Cooper shook himself. "Did we pass out?"

My fork was still in my hand. I lifted it to my mouth and touched my tongue to the pulled pork. "The food is cold."

He put his hand over his food like he was taking its temperature. "Mine too."

I rested the fork on the side of the plate. "Did I have some kind of magical accident?" Could my own magic have somehow reacted to the witch magic and caused me to blow a supernatural fuse?

He squinted at me. "How could us blacking out have been your fault? We were passed out, not frozen."

I pulled the pouch out from under my T-shirt. "I had the witches make this for me as a protection against nightmares. I'm just wondering if witchcraft and winter magic might be like baking soda and vinegar. You know, maybe the two being too close together caused something to happen."

"I don't think your magic and witchcraft work like that." He looked at his watch. "We were out for almost three hours."

"Wow, that's a long time. How on earth is that possible? Sanders is capable, but he wouldn't have done that." Then it hit me. "But Luna would have. She must have wanted to show me that she was more powerful than I was. That the witches' magic was no match for her powers."

"But wouldn't we have had nightmares?"

"Not me." I touched the pouch again. "Not if this was working right. And she knew about it, so she had to do something different."

"But I didn't have any magic protecting me, so I could have had nightmares. And I didn't."

"Then I don't know." I put my hands flat on the table. "This doesn't make any sense. If she didn't knock us out, then who did? Again, Sanders is certainly powerful enough to do it, but why would he?"

"Maybe we weren't the only ones affected. Give me a sec." He pulled his phone out and called someone. "Robbie, it's Cooper. Did anything weird just happen at the station?" He nodded a few times and said, "Uh huh." Then, "Same here. Okay, thanks."

He hung up. "It wasn't just us. Everyone at the station got knocked out too."

"Okay, this is beyond weird. Even for this town." I

got up from the table. "We need to figure out what's happening, and the only way I can think to do that is to talk to Sanders. But first I'm going to check on Juniper, Buttercup, and Holly."

"Good idea." He got up and went with me.

I knocked on the doors of my friends and employees, then stood back to see who'd answer first. Buttercup won. She was wearing a headset with a slim black mic that curved around her cheek, and carrying a game controller. And true to her style, she wore Mario Brothers pajama pants and a Labyrinth T-shirt.

"Hey." She was wide-eyed and chewing her lip as she stepped into the hall. "Something weird just happened to me."

"Us too."

Holly opened her door and peeked out. She looked worried. "H-hey."

I felt for her. "Did you just take an involuntary nap?"

Her eyes widened. "Yes. How did you know?"

"It happened to all of us." Juniper still hadn't answered so I knocked again.

"She's at Pete's," Buttercup said. "Probably just waking up. Because that's what happened, right? We all fell asleep."

"Yes," Cooper said. "That's exactly what happened."

"Why?" Buttercup asked.

I shook my head. "That's what we'd like to know. I'm going upstairs to talk to Sanders right now. Do either of you want to come?"

Holly shook her head. "No. He intimidates me.

Sorry."

"No problem. See you in the morning." He intimidated me, too, now that I'd seen him angry. As Holly closed her door, I turned to Buttercup. "What about you?"

"No can do. My guild is mad at me because I've been non-responsive for the last three hours and we were in the middle of a raid. I need to come up with a believable excuse."

I looked at her. "Any of them live in Nocturne Falls?"

"Nope. Osaka, Detroit, San Diego, Toronto…they're all over, but none in town."

And none of them had been asleep. Interesting.

"Tell them there was a gas leak in the building and you had to evacuate," Cooper said. "Orders of the fire department."

Buttercup smiled. "Okay, that should work. Thanks."

"You're welcome," he said. As she went back inside, he tipped his head toward the elevator. "You want my company or would you rather talk to Sanders alone?"

"I'd be happy to have your company." Whatever had happened, Cooper might as well find out with me. And having him along would boost my courage. Safety in numbers and all that—not that I thought Sanders had been behind the strange nap. I just wasn't sure how he'd take to being questioned about it.

We rode the elevator up to the third floor. At the company suite, I knocked on the door. I had to knock a second time before Olive finally answered. She was in a bathrobe and her hair was loose and a little messy.

"Sorry to wake you," I said.

"Sorry to be asleep. That wasn't my plan. This was my first night off in a long time and I was finally going to finish the book I've been trying to read all year, but I apparently drifted off a few pages in." She frowned. "Not often I get a night to myself."

I felt for her, I really did. "I can imagine. And again, I'm sorry to disturb you, but I need to speak to Sanders."

She smoothed her hair behind her ears. "Can I ask what this is about? He doesn't like to be woken up."

If she'd been asleep, she had no idea what had just happened. I wasn't in the mood to explain myself twice. "Please just get him and then I'll fill you both in."

She yawned, then nodded. "All right. Give me a few minutes. Like I said, he won't be happy."

She shut the door. Cooper and I looked at each other. I shrugged. "I really hope he can explain this."

"And if he can't? If he wasn't the one who caused it?"

"Then...I guess we assume it was Luna. Maybe the witches know something. Or have a way of pinpointing who was behind the magic that made us all sleep."

The door opened and Olive reappeared. "He's not here. He must still be out with Luna."

Even better. If she'd done something, he'd know. "Call him. This is important."

She sighed. "Let me get my phone." She wandered off again, this time leaving the door open. She returned with the phone in her hand but she was shaking her head, a very perturbed expression on her face. "He's not answering. I told you that woman was trouble. She probably asked him to turn it off."

I glanced at Cooper as a new thought formed in my head. "If he's that deep into his date with Luna, would he have done something like that?"

Cooper shrugged. "I have no idea."

"Done something like what?" Olive asked.

I had no choice but to tell her now. "I guess you wouldn't know this because you were sleeping, but for the last three hours, most of us have been asleep."

Her eyes narrowed and she just stared at me. "So have I. I don't follow."

"We've been asleep against our will. And when I say most of us, I mean probably the whole town." Sure, all I really knew was the firehouse, myself, Cooper, Holly, and Buttercup, but I had said probably.

She looked confused. "I still don't know what you're getting at."

"We were involuntarily asleep. Something, or more likely someone, knocked us out with some kind of magic or spell. And I'm here because I want to ask Sanders about it. If anyone could do something like that, it's the Sandman."

Her mouth opened and she nodded like realization had just struck. "Of course. Huh. I don't know what to tell you. He's out with Luna, so…" Her mouth firmed into a hard line. "He's out with Luna. And probably wanted to be alone with her, so he put everyone in town to sleep."

I frowned. "Would he do that?"

"Under her influence? He'd do just about anything. Or he might just be showing off for her. Either way, it's a good example of why I didn't want her around."

"Great," Cooper muttered.

"I know," Olive answered. "But no one ever listens to me."

I raised my brows. "I couldn't exactly forbid him to see her."

Olive raised a hand. "I understand, I do, but I said she was bad news and now this. Just proves my point is all."

I wasn't sure what to say to that. And I wasn't going to apologize for doing my job the way I saw fit. "I guess we'll see you in the morning. I can wait to talk to him until then, but I *will* be talking to him about this. He can't just knock the whole town out and think it's okay."

She hmphed. "Good luck making him see it that way."

"I'm sure it won't be easy, but I'm going to say what I have to say."

She nodded. "Good for you. See you in the morning."

As she closed the door, I turned to Cooper. "So our date was interrupted because of his date."

"I don't like it," he said. "It's an abuse of his power. You should tell your father about this. Can you imagine the havoc this has caused in town? The Ellinghams aren't going to be happy."

"No, I don't suppose they will be. Maybe Sanders will apologize." But I doubted it. I sighed. Sanders' visit was becoming one of my least favorite things that had happened since I'd become manager. And that was saying something. "How about I pack that barbeque into the fridge and we eat it tomorrow night? It'll heat up. In fact, you can do it with your summer elf magic. Right now, all I want to do is go to bed."

He slipped his arm around my waist. "Sounds good to me. C'mon, I'll help you clean up."

By the time the food was put away and I'd kissed Cooper goodnight (more than once, which is why it took so long), I was ready for everything to get back to normal. I changed into my pajamas, scooped Spider into my arms and headed for bed.

As tired as I was, I couldn't quite sleep. I grabbed my e-reader and flipped through the books I'd downloaded, finally landing on a juicy murder mystery I'd been meaning to get to.

The book was good. So good that I lost track of time, and when I came up for air it was nearly two in the morning. "Snowballs."

I had *not* meant to read that long, but I hadn't gotten sleepy. I turned the e-reader off, set it next to my phone on my nightstand and closed my eyes. But sleep didn't come. I was wide awake. Exhausted, but not sleepy. What was going on? I'd never had insomnia. Was this it? Must have been the stress of the day.

Spider was snoring softly at the bottom of the bed. Clearly, he wasn't having sleep issues. The little bugger. I sighed loudly and tried to sleep again.

An hour went by. I know because I checked the

time on my phone twice. Then I played games on my phone (leveled up twice in Candy Crush, thank you very much) until I ran out of lives, then logged onto Facebook to see if reading through the news feed would finally make me tired.

It didn't.

When I couldn't take being in bed and not sleeping anymore, I got up and went out to the living room and turned on the Home Shopping channel. I made myself a peanut butter and marshmallow fluff sandwich (with some rainbow sprinkles for crunch) and took it to the couch. I grabbed the throw off the back and tucked myself in. I figured the combination of carbs and the drone of voices ought to get me snoring. But by the time my sandwich was gone, everything they were selling had started to sound really good and I was more wide awake than ever.

This wasn't good. I changed the channel, putting on an old black and white movie. I lay down again to get comfy. Yep, this would definitely make me sleepy.

Except nope.

I stared at the screen, oddly invested in whether or not the chorus girl got the part *and* the guy.

Spider joined me, curling up in front of me where I lay. It was sweet, but I knew he wanted belly rubs. I obliged. What else was I going to do?

A knock at my window nearly startled me off the couch. The light from the television made it impossible to see but there was only one person who thought my fire escape doubled as a door.

Greyson.

I got up to open the window, careful not to disturb

Spider. "You realize showing up on my fire escape at this hour could qualify you as a stalker."

His eyes gleamed with amusement. "I saw the light of the television. I wouldn't have come up if you weren't awake."

"Maybe Spider was watching it."

He squinted. "Your cat watches TV?"

"No." I gave him a look. My patience was thinning with the lack of sleep. "What's up?"

He gave my pajamas a once over before answering. "Nothing. I just saw you were up so I thought I'd see if everything was okay. Is it?"

That was sweet of him. I felt bad I'd been a little cross. "Yeah, I guess. Just can't sleep."

"There's a lot of that going around tonight."

"Really? That's odd. But then maybe it isn't. I don't know what's what anymore." I ran my fingers over the neck of my top, catching them on the ribbon holding the magic pouch. "Hey, you don't think that the stuff the witches used in the nightmare protection spell could be keeping me awake, do you?"

"I don't think so. But I guess anything is possible."

I leaned against the window. I should invite him in, but then that might really end my chance of sleep. "You said a lot of other people weren't sleeping tonight? How do you know? You go around looking in a lot of windows?"

He laughed. "No. I've just seen a lot of lights on tonight that I don't normally."

What the tundra was going on? More of Sanders' tricks? "Normally? Are you usually up all night? I mean, I know you're a vampire but you have to sleep sometime—and since you're also up during the day, I just figured you were on more standard human hours."

"Not exactly. Vampires don't need the same amount of sleep as most supernaturals. When I do sleep, it tends to be during daylight hours. Even though I can daywalk, being awake when the sun is up never feels completely right."

"I see. Well, you really must not need to sleep after that three-hour nap we all had earlier."

His expression screwed up into a question. "What three-hour nap?"

Greyson wasn't a kidder, but I still had to ask. "You're teasing me, right?"

"No. I really don't know what you mean."

I blinked at him. "The whole town blacked out this evening from about seven to ten, most likely due to Sanders wanting 'alone time' with Luna. How were you the special snowflake who stayed awake?"

He did a little random pointing thing with his index finger. "You remember that conversation we just had about daysleep and how vampires aren't like other supernaturals when it comes to that sort of thing?"

"Yes, but..." My exhausted brain struggled to catch up. "So are you saying that Sanders' powers don't extend to you? That you can't be influenced by him the way humans and apparently elves and other supernaturals are?" If that was true, maybe the Ellinghams didn't know about the Big Nap either. Which could work in my favor. At least temporarily.

"That's exactly what I'm saying. Being dead has all

kinds of advantages. A vampire's sleep cycle is ruled by the rise and set of the sun." He shifted a little. "The magic that protects me from the sun also makes it possible for me to ignore the standard vampire coma that comes with it."

"How about that. Did you know the whole town was asleep during that time?"

"No. I was running Lucien's errand."

"Ah, yes, the elusive errand." I held my hand up. "Don't worry, I won't ask what it was."

"At least I can tell you what I was doing now that you know about him."

"Yes, that makes it so much better." I rolled my eyes. "If you had been here, would you have known the whole town was asleep?"

He shrugged. "Not unless I'd left my house. Of course I did, which is how I know there are an unusual number of people either up very early or unable to sleep."

My theory about the Ellinghams not knowing was looking more and more plausible. I hoped that would buy me some time to figure out what had happened with the nap and the current sleeplessness, and if it was Sanders' fault, get him to apologize. And then I hoped that would be enough for the Ellinghams to let it slide. After all, I couldn't be responsible for everything Sanders did. But if it was Luna's doing, well, the Ellinghams could do whatever they wanted with her. "You want to come in? I'm clearly not going to sleep."

"Sure." He slipped through the open window.

My stomach growled. "Maybe I should just fix breakfast. I didn't get to eat last night." That sandwich totally didn't count.

Greyson's eyes widened. "*You* didn't eat?" He put his hand on my forehead. "Are you well? Perhaps we should get you to the hospital—"

I pushed his hand away. "Yes, ha ha, very funny. But I'm starving now. Let me rummage around and see what I can come up with."

"You want to go to Mummy's? Let someone else do the work? Or we could order and get it delivered."

I stopped in my tracks. Mummy's would always be my first option for breakfast. "I'd love to go, but it's a little early for that, don't you think?"

He looked at his watch. "It's ten to six. By the time you change and we walk there, they'll be serving all the pancakes you can eat."

My mouth fell open. "It's almost six in the morning?"

"Yes."

I groaned. "I haven't slept a wink other than that stupid nap. Today is going to be rough."

"Good thing they serve coffee." He tipped his head at me. "Are you sure you want to go? I'm okay getting delivery."

"No, the walk and the fresh air will do me good. Maybe wake me up enough not to completely lose it on Sanders when I talk to him in a couple hours. Give me a few minutes to pull myself together."

"I'll wait right here."

I went to brush my teeth, pull my hair into a ponytail and change. Nothing complicated, just jeans, a T-shirt, and my leather jacket. The weather was finally cool enough for fall clothes and I couldn't be happier.

I liked the warm weather of Georgia, but as Christmas approached, I wanted the cold. It felt like home.

I kissed Spider on the head and picked up my purse. "I'm not in any mood to jump off the fire escape so you can either take the elevator with me, or I'll meet you on the sidewalk."

He put his arm around my waist. "The elevator it is."

Mummy's was busy. At least it seemed busy, but I'd never been there at six in the morning before, so maybe it was always like that when the place opened. Didn't matter, we got a booth and settled in. Most of the faces around us looked as tired as I felt. The town-wide insomnia seemed like a very real thing.

Reena, our server, brought us a carafe of coffee and left it like she knew I was in bad shape. Or maybe I looked that awful. I was beyond caring. And while I normally would have skipped the coffee in favor of a Dr Pepper, today was going to require more caffeine than the doctor could deliver. I poured a cup, dumped in a bunch of sugar and a big glug of cream, and stirred.

Greyson watched, a mix of amusement and pity in his eyes. "You going to be okay?"

"What choice do I have?" I sipped the coffee. It wasn't half bad with all that sugar and cream. "It's just a lack of sleep, it's not like I'm dying or anything. I'll make it through the day. I'm not going to abandon my employees. They're probably just as sleepy as I am." Although I might have to cancel on Cooper in favor of a very early bedtime.

Reena came back. "You kids ready to order?"

Greyson being called a kid made me smile and instantly lightened my mood. I opened my menu, even though I didn't need it to know what I wanted. "Blueberry pancakes, extra syrup."

"Tall or short stack?"

"Tall. Side of bacon, too."

"You got it." She turned to Greyson. "And for you, hon?"

"Steak and eggs. Rare and over easy."

"Biscuits, toast or cinnamon roll?"

He looked at me and smiled. "Cinnamon roll."

She nodded and took our menus, tucking them under her arm. "I'll get that right in."

"Reena?" I asked.

She stopped. "Something else for you, hon?"

"I was just wondering. How did you sleep last night?"

She snorted. "Like a baby. I was at my sister's last night and the book club turned into box-of-wine club, if you know what I mean. Ended up passed out on her couch. Almost missed my shift this morning."

As far as I could tell, Reena was human, so maybe not everyone had been affected by the insomnia. "Does your sister live in town?"

"No, she lives over in Bridgerton."

Greyson cleared his throat softly. "The next town over."

I smiled at her. "Thanks, Reena. Sounds like you had a fun night."

"That we did." She patted her hand on the table. "I'll just run that order into the kitchen."

I slumped in my seat as she left. "This isn't good.

If the whole town couldn't sleep, people are going to be seriously cranky. And there's no way the Ellinghams won't hear about it."

"They won't blame you. It's not your fault."

"Not directly, but Sanders is here because of the store and that makes him at least partially my responsibility. Even if Luna is behind all this, it's kind of the same thing. She's here because of him." I exhaled hard and stared at the ceiling. "I hope he tells me the truth this morning."

"You think he won't?"

I looked at Greyson again. "I have no idea."

Half a carafe of coffee and a very large stack of pancakes later, I was feeling better about confronting Sanders. It didn't hurt that Greyson had volunteered to come with me. I'd thought about waiting until eight, but the sooner I got to the bottom of this mess, the better.

Which is how I came to knock on Sanders' door at seven fifteen in the morning. I braced myself for an unhappy Olive and an even crankier Sanders, but they were just going to have to deal.

Unless, of course, they never answered the door. I knocked again. Greyson leaned on the wall and cocked an eyebrow. "Heavy sleepers."

"Apparently."

"I was being sarcastic." He tipped his head toward the apartment. "There's no one inside."

I frowned at him. "How do you know?"

He tapped his ear. "No heartbeats."

"Oh. Wait, maybe you can't hear Sanders' since

he's not a regular supernatural."

"I could hear him in the shop yesterday. His pulse has a very slow, distinct rhythm to it. Like a metronome. Trust me, he's not in the apartment."

"Snowballs. If he left early because he didn't want to deal with me..." My mood took a turn for the cranky. I tried the knob. Locked. "I'm going in."

Greyson straightened. "I figured you had a key."

"I do, in my office, but I'm not taking the time to go down there and get it."

His brow wrinkled. "What are you going to do?"

"Give me a sec." I took a breath, called up my magic and slipped under the door. I materialized flat against it and kept my eyes closed for a moment. I'd figured out a while back that keeping them shut gave me the shortest recovery time after the wobbliness of the Saint Nick Slide.

After a few seconds, I opened them and found a spot to fix my eyes on to make sure the dizziness was all gone. The spot I chose was a small, black dot on the floor.

As the dot came into focus, I realized what it was.

A spider. A curled-up, dead spider.

Luna. There was no real reason to think her name, but that's all that filled my head. Well, her name and the muted clanging of a distant warning bell. I took a look around and the clanging got louder. The apartment was a disaster. Not the kind of mess it had been after Sanders' hourglass went missing or the kind of wreck that followed a party or a particularly messy guest, but the kind of chaos that was the remains of a break-in.

Or a fight.

I unlocked the door to let Greyson in.

He stared at me from the other side. "What was that?"

"Just something I can do." Now wasn't the time to explain. "Something's wrong. Look around."

He took a few steps in and let out a low whistle. "I'd say. Sanders ought to treat guest quarters with more respect."

"Actually, I was thinking there was a serious throw-down in here."

"I could see that too." He glanced at me. "What else are you thinking?"

"That Luna Nyx is involved in this."

"I don't know. Sanders was awfully lovey-dovey with her to put up a fight if she wanted him to go somewhere."

"Agreed. But Olive wouldn't have gone willingly, and she's not here either. You said so yourself. For Sanders to run off with his ex is one thing, but for Olive to have gotten stuck in the middle of it, and possibly had something done to her against her will, now that's another thing entirely. I like Olive. She's a hard worker and for as much as she does for Sanders, she doesn't deserve to have anything bad happen to her."

"I agree, but we might be jumping to conclusions here. For all we know Sanders is just exceptionally messy and Olive is off running an errand for him."

"Then is this just a coincidence?" I bent down, tamped down my aversion to such things, and picked up the spider. I held it out to Greyson on the flat of my palm. "I mean, maybe it's just a dead spider."

His brows lifted and then he shook his head. "And maybe it's not."

"We should call the sheriff, get something official going," Greyson said.

"Sure, in a sec." I had another question first. "Do you smell blood?" I really needed the answer to be no.

His nostrils flared, then he shook his head. I exhaled in relief as he spoke. "There might have been a struggle but no blood was spilled. At least not here."

"Good." I deposited the spider onto the small entry table, happy not to have it in my hand anymore. "We should look around, see if we can find anything that might tell us where Luna took them or what her next step might be. Olive's a smart cookie; if she had a chance to leave a clue, she would have."

"I still think we need to call the sheriff."

"We do. And I will. In fact, how about while I do that, you go have a look through the rest of the apartment and see if you can find anything that might be a hint? Just be careful what you touch in case the sheriff wants to dust for prints. Or maybe that's not a thing since most supernaturals wouldn't have prints on file anyway."

"There are some. I'll keep my hands to myself just to be on the safe side." He headed toward the bedrooms while I dialed.

I'd put the sheriff's department on speed-dial a couple months ago. Really it was so I could get a hold of Birdie whenever I needed her. Mostly to answer questions and hit up Mummy's for breakfast with me. (I had serious respect for the woman's appetite.) I hadn't imagined I'd be calling her about a suspected kidnapping.

"Nocturne Falls Sheriff's Department, Sheriff Merrow speaking."

So much for getting Birdie. I guess it was a little early for her to be at her desk. But the sheriff was who I was trying to reach anyway. "Sheriff? It's Jayne Frost. I think there's been a kidnapping."

"Who's been kidnapped?"

I liked that he got right to it, but then Sheriff Merrow was not a man who made small talk regardless of the situation. "Tempus Sanders and his assistant, Olive Pine. Or maybe not Sanders at all, maybe just his assistant. I'm not sure, but something's not right. They should have been here and—"

"The Sandman?"

I took a breath and told myself to stop rambling. "Yes."

The sheriff muttered a curse before asking, "Where are you?"

"In the apartment the company keeps for special guests and corporate visits. It's where Sanders and his assistant are staying while they're here. Top floor of the building in back of the shop. Door's open."

"I know the apartments. On my way." He hung up.

I did the same and turned to see Greyson walking toward me. A thought occurred to me. "Any chance you saw Olive's messenger bag lying around?"

"No. That must have gone with her."

"I figured. Find anything else?"

"Enough to make me think the spider you found wasn't just a spider." He held out his hand. In it was a small sprig of black baby's breath.

"Where was it?"

"The smaller bedroom."

"Olive's room." This was getting worse by the second. "That proves Luna was here."

"It does. Doesn't mean she's the one who caused all this or the reason Sanders and Olive are missing, but it sure doesn't make her look innocent."

"But what reason would she have for being in Olive's room?"

Greyson added the baby's breath to the entry table, placing it next to the spider. "Nothing I can come up with. You get a hold of someone at the station?"

"The sheriff is on his way."

A knock sounded on the open door. I looked to see Kip standing there.

"Everything okay?" He yawned.

"Not really. Did you sleep last night?" I could guess the answer to that based on the dark circles under his eyes.

"No, and I feel awful."

"You're not alone." The insomnia might come in

handy. "Did you hear anything last night or early this morning? Sounds of a struggle maybe?"

He glanced past me at the apartment as he shook his head. "No. But I ended up watching movies all night and I had my headphones on." He made eye contact with me again. "I didn't want to be the reason anyone else couldn't sleep."

"Very considerate of you, but the sleeplessness was widespread."

That didn't seem to register as much as the mess behind me, which was all he seemed to be looking at. "What happened in there?"

I hesitated. "I'm not sure yet, but as of right now, Sanders and Olive are missing."

His eyes rounded. "Oh, wow. That's not good."

"No, it's not. And I don't mind you sharing that information with the other employees, but I'd really like to keep a lid on things. Now is not the time to start a bunch of wild rumors."

He nodded. "Wouldn't look good for any of us."

I was the only one the blame would fall on, but I appreciated the solidarity. "Right."

He rubbed at his eyes. "Well, let me know if I can do anything to help. Until it's time to open, I'll be in my apartment trying to wake myself up enough to make it through the day." He grimaced. "I mean, I'll be fine. I don't want you to think I'll be doing less than my best at work today."

"I know, Kip. And we're all dragging, so you're not in this alone." As he went back to his place, I returned to the chaos. Greyson was in the middle of the living room having a look around.

He crouched and peered closer at something. "That's interesting."

I took a few steps forward. "What is it?"

He picked up a broken twig, the remnant of a smashed flower arrangement, and poked at the thing. "Looks like a scrap of black silk. Like someone tore a piece of clothing."

"So more evidence that points at Luna."

He stood. "Seems that way."

"You and I need to pay a visit to—"

"Miss Frost?"

I twisted to see Sheriff Merrow behind me. That was fast, but the man *was* a werewolf, and for all I knew, he had run here. Then again, the sheriff's department was only a few blocks away. "Thank you for coming so quickly."

He nodded as he surveyed the apartment. Then he pinched the radio on his shoulder. "Deputy Blythe, I need you at the Santa's Workshop apartments, third floor. Bring an evidence kit."

The radio squawked with her reply. "Ten-four."

He pulled out a notepad and looked at me. "Tell me what you know. Start from the beginning."

By the time I had filled him in, Deputy Blythe had arrived with a heavy black canvas bag slung over one shoulder.

She greeted him with a jerk of her head. "Sheriff."

"Deputy. Possible kidnapping. Sweep the rooms."

She nodded. "Ransom note?"

"No," I answered. They both looked at me. "We had a little look around. Well, Greyson did."

Greyson held his hands up. "I didn't touch anything, but Jayne and I both found evidence that points to Luna Nyx as the perpetrator."

The sheriff's dark brows knit together. "What kind of evidence?"

I pointed to the spider and the dried flowers on the entry table. "A dead spider, then Greyson found that sprig of black baby's breath, which she had in her hair at the shop yesterday, and a piece of black silk, possibly from her dress."

Greyson pointed behind him. "Right here on the floor. I poked at it, but that's it."

The sheriff frowned. "At least you didn't touch it."

The sheriff might not be happy with us, but really, had he expected us just to stand there and wait? I figured I'd better share the rest of what I knew. "Also, I talked to Kip already. He's one of the employees who lives across the hall. He said he didn't hear any sounds of fighting. He's in 3B."

Sheriff Merrow's frown deepened. "I'll still need to talk to him. And whoever else lives on this floor."

"That would be Rowley Gladstone and his wife, Dorthea. They're in 3A. Only been here a week."

The sheriff made a note of that. "What about the rest of the employees?"

"Kip and Juniper work the opening shift, so they'll be on duty shortly. I haven't talked to Juniper. She lives on the floor below, same as I do. And so does Buttercup, who was probably gaming all night. Holly's probably still in her apartment downstairs. She and Buttercup work the evening shift and Rowley's mostly on the gap shift." I wasn't sure what other info the sheriff might need, but I knew he'd talk to all of them no matter what I said. "Are you done with Greyson and me?"

His eyes narrowed and I wasn't sure he'd heard my question. "If Sanders *was* kidnapped, would that explain why no one in my house slept last night? No sleep magic."

"None of us slept either, although I think it was confined to town limits." I told him about Reena.

"Interesting."

"I thought so too. And I don't know if the lack of sleep is related to Sanders and Olive being missing or not, but the two things would be awfully coincidental not to be."

"I'm not a big fan of coincidence, Miss Frost. Not in a town like this."

"I hear you." I waited a beat. "So, um, can Greyson and I…" I pointed my thumb toward the door.

"Yes, you can go. But don't go far and keep your phone on."

"Will do." I slanted my eyes at Greyson and tipped my head for him to come on.

Neither of us said a word until we were back in my apartment, and then I was the first to speak. "We have to go to the Black Rose *now*."

"You really think that's a good idea?"

"Yes." Spider wandered out from the bedroom, yawning. The show off. "We need to see if Luna's still there."

"And if she's not?"

"Then you can talk Edna Turnbuckle into letting us into her room. We might find something."

"We might. But now that the police are involved,

maybe we should leave that to them. And what if she is there? What then?"

"Then..." I wasn't sure. I reached down to pick Spider up. He really was the only spider I was interested in touching ever again. "Ask her how her date went last night? See if we can get her to tell us what happened? Figure out if she has any idea where Sanders and Olive are? Maybe she'll act guilty."

"I don't know. We could be tipping her off. Again, I think we should leave this to the police."

Spider head-butted me as I gave Greyson a stern look. "That really doesn't sound like you. All law-abiding and whatnot." It was downright Cooper-esque.

"I realize leaving it to the police isn't how I normally play things, but this is the Sandman we're talking about. I might be able to do without his brand of sleep, but very few can. This is bigger than both of us, Jayne. If Luna is involved in this and we spook her and she runs, we could really screw things up."

I sighed. "I suppose you're right."

His eyes sparkled. "But we could at least find out if she's still there."

I grinned. "What do you have in mind?"

He snorted. "Nothing dramatic. Just a phone call."

"Oh." I scratched Spider's chin. He tried to chew on my fingers. I could take a hint. "I guess that works."

While Greyson got his phone out, I went to work feeding Spider.

"Hello, I was trying to reach one of your guests, Luna Nyx. I'm a friend, yes." Greyson paused, listening. "I see. Thanks for letting me know. Have a good day."

I stood at the sink, rinsing out Spider's bowl. I looked over my shoulder. "Well?"

"Checked out late last night. And she wasn't happy."

I dumped a can of Chicken Party into the dish. "Isn't 'not happy' sort of her general look?"

"According to Edna Turnbuckle, Luna checked out in a huff and seemed weepy and angry. Edna's words."

I put the bowl on the floor and got out of the way as Spider dove in. I didn't want to lose a finger. "Really? You think she and Sanders had an argument? That could be what triggered all this. Maybe she proposed something that was more than he was willing to go along with, he rejected her, she got mad and, after checking out, decided if she couldn't have him, no one could."

Greyson leaned on the counter. "I'd buy that. But how does kidnapping Olive fit into the picture?"

I thought it over. "Luna checks out of the D&B, getting angrier and angrier. She goes to the apartment to confront Sanders, maybe to tell him off one more time. She gets there and Olive won't let her in. Won't let her see Sanders."

Greyson nodded. "She wasn't going to let us see him. I can only imagine what she would have said to Luna."

"Right. Luna's already mad, but Olive makes her furious. Plus she already knows Olive doesn't like her, and that's when everything freezes over. They fight, which is how the apartment gets wrecked, then Luna uses her magic to subdue them both and drag them off to who knows where."

What little color there was in Greyson's face vanished.

It was enough to give me pause. "What? Did I miss something?"

"If Luna really did use her magic to subdue them...her *reaper* magic..." He swallowed. "They might both be...dead."

A chill washed through me. More than a chill, it was a harsh, burning cold that sucked the breath out of my lungs. "That—that can't be right."

Greyson wiped a hand over his mouth. "It would explain why the town had insomnia last night. No Sandman, no sleep."

"Oh no. That can't be." I breathed open-mouthed, trying to catch my breath and wanting very much to find a hole in Greyson's logic. "It makes sense. Awful, horrible sense."

He just nodded, looking a little numb.

I sucked in another breath. "Wait, maybe it doesn't. If he really were dead, wouldn't the whole world be sleepless? It was only Nocturne Falls. As far as we know."

Greyson shrugged half-heartedly. "Maybe. Or maybe it's just the kind of thing that's going to spread across the world like a virus. Maybe tonight it'll be the whole state of Georgia that's sleepless. Tomorrow, the rest of the South."

I stared at him, my stomach in knots and my sleep-deprived brain struggling to process the possibilities. "Son of a nutcracker."

I couldn't just stand around doing nothing. "We have to go to the Black Rose and look through Luna's room. We might find something. I don't care if we have to break in to do it, either." I crossed my arms. "And if you don't want to come with me, I'll call Cooper." I wanted to text Cooper anyway to see how he and everyone at the firehouse was doing with the sleeplessness.

The mention of Cooper snapped Greyson out of it. He stopped staring into space to look at me. "No, I'll go. I'm sure we can talk Edna into it."

"Great. I'll get my—" My phone rang and we both jumped, proof of how unnerving this whole mess was. Not that unusual for me, but I'd never seen Greyson like this. I tapped the screen to answer. "Hello?"

"Miss Frost, this is Sheriff Merrow. I'm convening a meeting at the station in half an hour. I'd like you to be there."

"Did you find something?"

"Nothing beyond what you and Greyson uncovered, but meeting will give you a chance to explain what's happened so far to the rest of my team. Then we can make an informed decision together about our next steps."

Color me impressed. "I appreciate you keeping me in the loop like this. I wasn't expecting that."

"You were Sanders' main point of contact and your store is the reason he was in town in the first place. And this way you can keep your father and uncle informed as well. I know they'll want to be kept apprised of the situation."

I closed my eyes for a second as his words sank in. I still needed to call my dad. Yeti biscuits. That was not going to be fun. "Right. Okay, half an hour. I'm bringing Greyson with me and I'm inviting Cooper Sullivan, too."

"That's fine. My brother, Titus, will be here. I figure we may need some search parties so best we include him from the get-go."

"Works for me. See you soon." I hung up and started texting my favorite fireman. *Hope you're surviving without sleep. Can you meet me at the sheriff's department in 30?*

Greyson's eyes narrowed. "What are you inviting Cooper to?"

"A meeting at the sheriff's department." I hit send. "The sheriff is holding a meeting in thirty minutes to get everyone on the same page. You can be there, right?"

He made a curious face. "Of course. What else would I be doing?"

"Great, but…" I tried for a sympathetic smile. "I

need to shower and wake myself up."

"And you want some alone time to do that."

"You win." I gave him a thumbs-up, super happy that he was so perceptive. "Sorry, but this lack of sleep is making my fuse a little short and my head a little fuzzy. I need to be alone for a few minutes to think and get ready and chill."

"I understand." He kissed me on the cheek, then headed for the window. "See you there."

He slipped out and jumped over the fire escape. I closed and locked the window, watching him walk away on the street below for a moment. I was about to hit the shower when Cooper responded.

We're all dragging. The chief filled me in. I'll be at the meeting.

Good, I typed back. *See you there.*

Dr Pepper in hand, I headed for the shower. I cranked it on and stepped into the steam. The hot water helped tremendously, the caffeine slightly less, but I was more awake when I got out than when I'd stepped in.

I put on a new outfit. Black work pants, a silk tee, and a pinstriped blazer. Then I did some light makeup and twisted my hair into a cute, albeit slightly messy, up-do. A little jewelry and my sensible black heels, and I was ready. Hey, I'd have to go into the office at some point. Might as well prep for that now.

And, if I'm being perfectly honest, knowing that I was going to have to stand in front of a room full of deputies and first responders and give them the Sanders report was a little unnerving, especially when he'd gone missing on my watch. I wanted to look like

I knew what I was doing. Work clothes made me feel that way.

I filled Spider's dry food bowl, grabbed my purse, and was out the door. As I walked to the station, I made some mental notes about what I was going to say and what I would suggest happen next.

Examining Luna's room at the Black Rose was at the top of that list. I was convinced there had to be a clue there somewhere. Even if it wasn't a flashing neon sign that pointed us in the direction she'd gone, it could be enough to start us on the right path.

Birdie was behind the reception desk when I arrived at the station. Her back was to me as she bustled around, making coffee and piling paper napkins on top of a box of doughnuts, presumably for the meeting. "Be with you in a just a sec."

"Morning, Birdie."

She turned, her hands going skyward when she saw me. "Oh, Princess Jayne! I'd say good morning, but it isn't good, is it? I'm so sorry about Tempus and Olive going missing. Hank will find them. You'll see."

"I hope so." I rested my hands on the counter and restrained the urge to remind her not to call me Princess. I was kind of getting used to it, and I'd figured out a while back that Birdie was going to do whatever she wanted. "I just don't know how that's going to happen without any clues."

"Honey, we're werewolves." She tapped the side of her nose as the sheriff stepped out of his office. "Best trackers around."

He frowned as he stood in the doorway. "Except there doesn't seem to be a scent trail."

"What's that now?" Birdie looked at him, clearly perplexed. "What kind of creature doesn't leave a scent trail?"

He let out a dark, unhappy sound that was somewhere between a grunt and a sigh. "The three we're after, that's what kind." He studied me, nostrils twitching. "You don't have much of one either, unless you're wearing perfume. I'd ask if that was a trait of all winter elves, but I could scent your employees just fine this morning."

"About that...can I speak to you in your office? I might be able to shed some light on why that is." I hoped the privately part was implied. I didn't want Birdie to feel bad, but I also didn't want to tell the whole world what Sanders and Luna really were. Their status as elementals wasn't my information to share, but this was an extenuating circumstance to be sure. And Birdie wasn't known for keeping secrets.

I expected him to move, but he stayed right where he was. "You mean because they're elementals?"

My mouth came open, but for a few seconds, I had nothing to say. "I, uh, didn't know that was public knowledge."

"It's not. But when a visitor comes to town, especially someone as important as Tempus Sanders, we do our research. It's in the best interests of the town that the right people know who's headed our way."

"I see. So you already knew Sanders was an elemental?"

He nodded. "We did. Luna too. Also knew Luna showing up might be a possibility. Our research department is very thorough."

Birdie smiled and waved at me.

"You're the research department?"

"Some of it. I'm pretty good with the computer."

"She's excellent with that internet business," Sheriff Merrow added. "Downright scary with it, if you ask me."

I kind of knew about Birdie's skills already. I had used them on more than one occasion. "That still doesn't explain why Olive doesn't have a scent."

"I just figured she was an elemental, too."

"She's not. She's a winter elf." I almost said 'just like me,' but realized that would have been a half-truth.

Greyson walked through the door behind me, and nodded a greeting to us as the sheriff answered.

"Then maybe Luna had a way to cover Olive's tracks. She knew there were shifters in town, knew we could track them. Seems reasonable she would have taken precautions. She didn't get to be the Mistress of Nightmares by being sloppy."

"No, she got there by divorcing Sanders."

"But she's held onto the position for quite a few years now. That wouldn't happen if she was the kind to let details slide." He glanced toward the rear of the building. "Anyway, if you're ready, my team's assembled, and with Greyson here, that's all of us. We should get this meeting underway."

Birdie picked up the coffee carafe in one hand and the box of doughnuts in the other. "Right this way, Princess. Hank, bring that little stack of paper plates and my laptop."

"Aunt Birdie, we do not need refreshments for—"

200

"Don't be a sassmouth. Of course we need refreshments. We're working through a serious sleep deprivation issue here. And doughnuts and coffee make everything better."

He grunted something, picked up the plates and the laptop and walked toward the back of the station, muttering more things I couldn't quite make out.

It would have been amusing if not for the situation. There was so much going on in my head, I was a little lost in thought as I followed Birdie to the conference room. How were we going to find Sanders? Was he okay? Was Olive? Greyson stayed at my side, letting me ponder, but I snapped out of it when we walked into the room. Besides the three deputies, the room also held Titus, the fire chief, and Cooper. It was nice to see his friendly face.

Next to Deputy Blythe, a laptop sat open and someone else was video-conferenced in.

The sheriff pointed at the screen. "Deputy Lafitte is online with us as he's unable to be out during daylight hours."

Deputy Lafitte smiled and waved, showing off a set of pearly fangs. "Sorry I couldn't be there in person."

His voice had a rolling lilt that made for easy listening, but I didn't know enough to know where that accent came from. "No problem," I said, even though I wasn't sure he was talking to me.

The sheriff introduced me to everyone, but the only two I hadn't met yet were Deputy Cruz and Deputy Everly, both good-looking guys, which I was starting to think was a requirement for employment at the station. The good-looking part, not the guy part. That done, we all took seats as Birdie poured coffee and distributed doughnuts.

The sheriff nodded at me. "Miss Frost, go ahead and tell everyone what you told me at the apartment."

I ran through the story, same as I had before, starting from the beginning when Sanders and Olive had arrived, then running through the scene at Elenora's house, when Luna had shown up at the signing, how they'd made a date for that evening, how Sanders and Olive had gone missing, and finishing with the part about Luna's stay at the Black Rose. "She's checked out now, but I think someone should get over there and go through the room. See if anything's been left behind that might give us a clue where she's taken Sanders and Olive."

"*If* she's taken them," Deputy Blythe said.

"You think she didn't?" My tone probably could have been nicer, but my butt was on the line here. And I didn't have any idea who else might have done it if not Luna.

"I just think we need to keep our minds open." Deputy Blythe looked at the sheriff. "Everly and I can run that room down if you like."

He nodded. "Do it. Go now."

They got up from the table and left. Deputy Lafitte spoke as the door closed behind them. "Do you have pictures of Sanders and his assistant?"

Birdie started typing on her laptop. "I can help with that." She leaned back, tapped one button rather decisively and looked at Lafitte. "Check your email. I just sent you the picture from the book signing article in the Tombstone."

She swung the laptop around so we could all see it as well. There in living color was Sanders, smiling up from his table. Olive was more difficult to make out in the background, but she was there too.

"How tall is he?" Lafitte asked.

"Tall," I said. "Six six, maybe."

He stared at his phone where he had the picture open. "And he's a pretty big guy, too, right? Wide, I mean. But more round than muscle?"

I wondered where he was going with this. "Yes."

"And his assistant? She's a little harder to see."

"Petite in all ways. Short and slim."

Lafitte looked up. "During that three-hour nap you all took, I was wide awake. And I saw these two."

Everyone in the room swiveled to look at Lafitte.

I'd never been as happy about the town's vampire population as I was right now. "Where?"

"I was patrolling the neighborhoods on the west side of town. Like most nights, there wasn't much going on but I'd parked on Cauldron Lane to watch the Newtons' house for a bit. They're out of town. Anyway, I saw two people walking. I didn't see their faces but based on the physical description, it was Sanders and Pine."

The sheriff's gruff voice cut in. "What were they doing?"

"Just out for a stroll from the looks of it."

I leaned in. "Was Luna with them? She's a tall, slender woman who looks like Morticia Addams long-lost sister. She would have been in all black."

"Didn't see anyone else—fitting that description or otherwise—but I was seeing them through the trees of the Newtons' property line. They were two blocks away."

Gotta love that vampire eyesight. "What time was it?"

Lafitte thought for a moment. "Seven thirty, give or take a few minutes."

I looked at Cooper. "It was a few minutes after seven when we fell asleep."

He nodded. "It was."

Greyson tapped his long fingers on the table. "Where would they have been going? Sanders had a dinner date with Luna at seven forty-five. Would Olive have walked him there?"

I thought about that. "Maybe. I'm not sure. Where were they supposed to be eating?"

Birdie started typing again. "I'm looking into that."

"I can help you there," Greyson said. "I'm pretty sure they went to Café Claude. I gave Olive that recommendation at the shop. She seemed pretty receptive to it."

The sheriff stood. "If Sanders and Pine were out walking without Luna, it's possible the plans had changed and he was meeting her somewhere else. Somewhere that wouldn't have had the audience of Café Claude."

"Or," I said, lifting my finger, "she could have already gotten control of Sanders' hourglass in the scuffle at the apartment and been directing them with some kind of sleepwalking spell. Just because Deputy Lafitte didn't see her doesn't mean she wasn't behind them, moving them along."

The sheriff looked at Lafitte. "What road were they on?"

"Spellcaster. Headed north."

Sheriff Merrow nodded. "And if they'd kept going in a straight line—"

"They would have ended up at the Black Rose," Lafitte finished.

My gut was telling me that wasn't the right answer. Edna would have told Greyson if Luna had shown up with Tempus and Olive in tow.

Just then, the chief's radio squawked with a call. "Chief, come in."

Titus answered with the receiver on his shoulder. "I'm here."

"We have a potential kitchen fire at 1319 Sycamore and both engines are out at other calls."

"On my way. I have Sullivan with me." He gestured at Cooper. "Let's go." Then he looked at the sheriff. "Sorry, Hank. It's been a busy morning already. Lack of sleep is making people do stupid things. I'll check in when this is handled."

"Thanks, Titus."

Cooper nodded at me. "See you later, Jay."

"Okay. Be careful." As they left, I got to my feet to speak to the sheriff. "I assume you're going to the Black Rose?"

"Yes." He pointed at Cruz. "Head there now and I'll meet you in a few."

"You got it, boss." Cruz gave us a short salute as he left.

Greyson got up to stand beside me while I spoke to the sheriff. "Okay, while you and Cruz handle that, Greyson and I will go to Café Claude. Greyson has known Jacque Baptiste for years. We can find out if the date ever happened or not."

The sheriff hooked a thumb in his utility belt. "Good. Birdie, you keep doing what you're doing, running down any possible places Luna might have taken our missing pair."

"I'm on it." Birdie never looked up from the keyboard, even when she took a bite of her doughnut. "I have a call in to Lucien, too."

I whipped around to face her. "Birdie, that's brilliant. I want to talk to him too. Actually, I think I'll do that first. Let's go see him."

Greyson frowned. "What? Why would you do that?"

"Because if anyone ought to know how to find a reaper, it's another reaper. You can take me to him. Or don't. I know where he lives. We'll call on Jacque after I see him. Birdie, you want to come with me?"

She finally glanced up. "To see Lucien? Sure, I could say hi to Hattie."

"Good, let's go." I started for the door, knowing she'd follow me. She always did.

"Hang on just a tick," the sheriff said. "Birdie, you already have an assignment."

Greyson grabbed my hand. "And you're not going there alone. I get that you want to find Sanders, but I don't think Lucien is going to be able to help. Just because he and Luna are the same kind of elemental doesn't mean they have some secret tracking ability on each other."

"No, but he's more likely than anyone else to know where and how she might go to ground."

"That's what I was thinking," Birdie said. She was

halfway around the table, her nephew's words clearly falling on deaf ears.

Greyson growled softly. "Lucien isn't like anyone else. You know that already. You don't just drop in on him."

Sheriff Merrow nodded. "Agreed. Let Birdie talk to him by phone. From *here*. Much safer." He pointed at the laptop Birdie had just been working on. "Besides, you have research to do."

I stared at him. "You're assuming he's going to take her call. I'm assuming he won't."

Birdie gave him a look, picked up her cell phone and started dialing. "We'll see right now."

We stood there waiting until Birdie moved the phone closer to her mouth. "Hattie? Is Lucien there?" Birdie's gaze lifted to us and she shook her head. "I understand. You have a good day."

She hung up. "He won't come to the phone."

The sheriff sighed. "Fine. Cruz can handle the D&B and Greyson and I will go see Lucien."

Greyson relaxed. "That's good. Let's do that. He'll definitely see me. But it can wait until Jayne and I check in with Jacque. I happen to know he's in the restaurant at five a.m. every morning anyway to make the day's bread. Lucien, on the other hand, is not even remotely a morning person. The fact that he's been unable to sleep won't have left him in a very good mood."

I snorted softly. "Is he ever in a good mood?"

Greyson's eyes narrowed. "My point exactly. Let's go see Jacque."

I relented and on the way to Café Claude, I made

Greyson call the restaurant to make sure Jacque was there. He was. And he was willing to take a break from baking to talk to us. Probably because of Greyson, because while Jacque liked me, Greyson was one of his best friends.

Jacque Baptiste was an incredible chef, but he was also a voyante, a kind of clairvoyant who sometimes got glimpses into the future. He'd had a vision about me once that had turned out to be spot on, so I was hoping he might have some insight into what was happening now, beyond whether or not Luna and Tempus had eaten dinner there.

The front of the restaurant was dark, but there were lights on in the back where the kitchen was. The door was locked, so I rapped my knuckles gently on the glass.

Greyson opened it. From the inside. I hadn't even seen him break away from me. "How did you get in here?"

"Back door. Jacque said he'd leave it open for me."

"Nice of him." I walked in and he locked the door behind me. "Where is he?"

"On the phone with his brother in France. He'll be out as soon as he hangs up."

A minute later, the lights came on in the dining room and Jacque walked out from the back. "Jayne, good to see you." He embraced me, kissing both my cheeks.

"Thank you for letting us come by and interrupt your morning."

"Of course."

"Can I ask if you fell asleep last night between

seven and ten?"

"Oui!" He threw his hands up. "I was just speaking with my brother in Marseille about it. What a strange thing!"

Greyson rocked back on his heels. "It was very strange indeed. What happened in the restaurant during that time?"

Jacque sighed. "All my customers went to sleep too. As soon as we all woke up, they left and I sent most of my staff home, then I went home to check on Claude. He was fine."

Claude was his little dog and the café's namesake. I looked around. The tables still held plates of unfinished food. "That explains the state of your dining room."

He threw his hands up and muttered a few words in French. "I cleaned the kitchen on my own, but that's it so far. The bread had to be made. My staff is coming in early to help. They wanted to check on their families just like I wanted to make sure Claude was all right. I couldn't say no." He let out a long, heavy sigh. "But I had a dream while I was asleep. A vision."

This was what I'd been hoping for. "What was it, Jacque? Please tell me. I need to know if it can help me."

He shook his head slowly. "I don't want to tell you, Princess. It is not a good thing."

Snowballs. I braced myself for the worst. "That's okay, I just need to know. A very important man is in danger. A man who's been a guest of mine. Well, a guest of the shop's, but that makes him my responsibility."

MISS FROST SAVES THE SANDMAN

Jacque's brows lifted. "The Sandman? He was supposed to eat here, but he never did."

That cleared up one question, but I needed to know about Jacque's vision more than anything else right now. "Yes, that's who's in danger, so please tell me, whatever you saw. It might help me save him before it's too late."

Jacque's breath hissed out between his teeth. "Princess Jayne, I saw death."

For a second, my heart stopped. Then I laughed. Jacque's vision just confirmed what we already knew. "Of course you did. His ex-wife is a grim reaper. And we're pretty sure she's the one who's kidnapped him. In fact, my next question is going to be if she showed up for the reservation last night."

"No, she did not," Jacque said. "But the death I saw was not a person. It was a feeling." He held his hands out in front of him like he was holding a big ball. "It surrounded everything. Like a shroud."

My heart stopped beating again. "Are you saying the Sandman was dead?"

He hesitated. "Not in my vision. But what I saw was a narrow slice of time. And that time was running out."

Of course time was running out. Sanders was the Sandman. He could, in small increments, control time through sleep. Except maybe Luna controlled it now, if she had his hourglass. I understood why she might want to hurt Olive, but why would she want to do Sanders harm?

Unless the whole I-still-love-you-and-want-to-get-back-together thing had been a big act. What if she just wanted revenge on him for breaking her heart?

This whole thing was starting to smell worse than a wet yeti.

"I have to find them and get them away from her *now*. If she hurts Olive or Sanders—or does something worse than just hurt them—the world will be in chaos. Can you imagine the Mistress of Nightmares in charge of everyone's sleep?"

Greyson put his hand on my arm. "We'll figure this out. I'll contact the Ellinghams and—"

"Hang on," I turned back to Jacque. "Sanders and Luna never arrived for dinner, correct?"

Jacque shook his head. "They had a reservation, but they never showed. Never called to cancel either, but they weren't alone. None of our reservations showed. The sudden sleep created havoc. I didn't think anything of it."

"No, why would you?" I looked at Greyson. "Luna still could have met him here. And Olive certainly could have been with him. We already know she wasn't asleep when everyone else was. Then Luna could have put them under her spell and marched them off to who knows where. Maybe tossed them into her car and driven away. That has to be what happened. They could be miles away by now. What does she drive, by the way?"

"Black SUV. She pointed it out in the parking lot of the Black Rose when I walked her back there. She made a comment about how hard she thought it would be to find parking in town for a car that size. But if it happened that way, how do you explain the mess in the apartment?"

I gave that a few more seconds of thought. "She went there after Sanders and Olive were incapacitated. She must have been looking for something. Maybe Sanders was smart enough not to bring his hourglass."

"Maybe. That would explain it."

I stared out the front windows. The daylight was almost painful on my tired eyes. "Someone had to have seen something."

"Not if they were asleep."

"Snowballs. I keep forgetting that. I guess we're lucky Lafitte was on duty to see anything at all." My phone buzzed. I pulled it out of my purse and checked the screen. A text from Cooper. "Excuse me a moment."

How's it going?

All right, I texted back. *S & L never showed at the café.*

They could be farther away than we realize.

I know. Where are you headed now?

Back to the department with the chief to check in with Birdie.

Ok. Let me know if anything new happens. I looked up at the two men in front of me. I wasn't really sure what to do next. What I wanted to do was figure out where Luna had taken Sanders. But how? And I still needed to let my dad know what had happened, but I was dreading that so hard. "I should probably go back to the shop. I have to call my dad, and I'm at a dead end here."

"I'll walk you," Greyson said.

"Okay." I smiled at Jacque. "Thanks for seeing us. If you hear anything you think might help, or have another vision, please don't hesitate to call me. Even if it's not good news."

Jacque nodded. "Right away. Now I must return to my baguettes."

"See you soon."

He headed back to the kitchen.

We went out the front door, passing one of Jacque's servers. I was happy to see him. I hated to think of Jacque having to clean up the evening's mess by himself.

A block away from the restaurant, Greyson

nudged me with his elbow. "You going to be all right at work today?"

"I'll be fine." My anger would keep me awake.

"You don't sound fine. Is it just because you're tired?"

"No." I chewed on the inside of my cheek, so frustrated I could spit. "Sanders and Olive are in this mess because they came here. They were my responsibility. I should have done something."

"Like what?" Greyson asked. "He might have been your guest at the store, but he's also a grown man. It was his decision to re-engage with Luna."

"Yeah, but Olive told me not to trust Luna and now look."

"Seriously, what could you have done? Forbid him to go? You know that wouldn't have worked. If anything, it might have made him angry. And he knew better than any of us what he was getting into."

"Maybe. But it doesn't make me feel any better." I huffed out a breath. "What am I going to do?"

"We'll find him."

"How? I'm at a loss." I shoved a hand through my hair. I hated the feeling of helplessness.

A soft buzz vibrated out of Greyson's jacket.

"Hang on." Greyson stopped and stepped off to the side near a storefront. I went with him. He took his phone out and answered it. I leaned against him, putting my forehead on his shoulder while I listened to his side of the call. "Hello, Hugh. Yes, I know. No, it's not a good situation." A few breaths went by. "I figured he'd bring you up to speed. She's with me now. Walking her back to the shop. No. No. I'll keep you posted. Anything you can do to help would be great."

While he listened some more, I sighed into the fabric of his jacket. I knew someone had to have told the Ellinghams what was going on. They essentially owned the town and were about as powerful and influential as a family of vampires could be, but the truth was, no one was going to be able to help with this. This was beyond the scope of all of us.

Worst of all, my father was going to freak, and my uncle was going to freak even more. Christmas Eve didn't really happen without the Sandman's help.

Would they fire me? I hoped not. But I'd probably fire me. I'd at least place me on probation.

Maybe I wasn't cut out for this job. Maybe I should stick to being the Winter Princess. Go home to the North Pole and just accept I wasn't ever going to be more than next in line for the Winter Throne.

Okay, so that wasn't exactly a small thing. The Winter Throne was a powerful position. We controlled winter, after all. But I loved this town. And this job. And the life I'd made here. Besides Cooper and Greyson, I had friends who didn't let my royal status affect how they treated me.

That was priceless. I sure as snowflakes wasn't ready to leave any of this behind.

I straightened up. Time to end this pity party and do whatever I could to make things right. I wasn't a quitter and I wasn't going down without a fight. I couldn't put off telling my father any longer. Whatever happened, happened.

Even if that meant my dad came to Nocturne Falls.

"Absolutely." Greyson hung up.

I looked at him. "Well?"

"The Ellinghams are all aware of what's going on and they've reached out to all the resources they have. Which are substantial."

But it still probably wouldn't help. Call it a hunch, but that's what my gut told me. I just nodded and said, "Great. I really need to get home and call my dad. And you really need to get back to the station and head to Lucien's with Sheriff Merrow. I can walk the rest of the way on my own."

His brow wrinkled. "Are you ditching me again?"

I smiled as brightly as I could manage. "Try not to take it personally."

He didn't. At least it didn't seem like it when he kissed me goodbye.

If not for my sensible heels (which really weren't that sensible, seeing as how they were still heels), I would have run back to the warehouse. All I could think about was getting this call with my dad over. Getting that weight off my shoulders, no matter what the outcome, would be one less thing for me to worry about.

I went into the shop first to check on Kip and Juniper. They seemed to be doing all right, and thankfully, it was a little on the slow side. "I'll be in my office but I don't want to be disturbed for a bit. I have to check in with my father."

The looks on their faces told me they understood and sympathized.

I walked back to my office, trying to find the right words to tell him what had happened. I closed my door, sat down at my desk, and pulled out the container of eggnog fudge from the bottom drawer.

I ate two pieces while I thought, but the sugar wasn't helping as much as I'd hoped.

This was going to be a rip-the-bandage-off kind of situation. I would need to just come out with it.

I took a breath, picked up the globe, and gave it a shake.

He answered in record time. Or maybe it just felt like that.

I forced a smile I didn't feel. "Hi, Dad."

"Hi, honey." He was in his office. Probably calculating how many more copies of *Hush, Little Baby* to print for Christmas. "How did it go this morning? No complications with Sanders' departure, I hope."

I inhaled and exhaled before answering, reminding myself that there was no point in dragging this out. "About that...there's been some trouble. Sanders and Olive are missing. And we think Luna Nyx has kidnapped them. In fact, she's probably already in control of his hourglass based on some of the sleep-related nonsense that's been going on here."

My father sat dead still, staring at me. For a minute, I thought the globe had frozen up, then I realized he was processing the fabulous news I'd just delivered. Finally he blinked. "Missing? Kidnapped? Back up and start from the beginning."

No yelling. Maybe he was in shock. Well, hearing

the whole story ought to snap him out of that.

I laid the whole thing out just as I'd done for the police. Then I shrugged. "And that's it. We're doing what we can, but with the town knocked out while all of this went down, Luna could have taken them anywhere by now."

A sudden thought occurred to me. "You know, I'm not sure Luna bargained on Olive. I mean, kidnapping Sanders? That might have been planned. Or maybe not. But I don't think she would have willingly taken Olive too. They're not exactly best friends."

Wisps of icy vapor swirled off my father, a sure sign of his unhappiness (as were his arched brows and frown). I felt bad for the northern areas of the world. Someone was getting a blizzard tonight. Some freezing rain, at the very least. He pounded his fist on the desk in front of him. "How in the hell did this happen?"

That was more of the reaction I'd been expecting. A strange sense of relief swept through me. "I don't know. I'm sorry, Dad. I really am. Olive said Luna was bad news, but I didn't do anything about it. Not much, anyway. She came to visit Sanders at the second signing and I let her. I'm not sure what I could have done differently, but I probably could have come up with something if I'd just given it more thought. I know I've disappointed you and Uncle Kris. Whatever you decide to do, I'm not going to argue. Even if it means I get fired."

My father's mouth opened and I braced myself for the bad news. "Fire you? Yes, this is awful, terrible, disappointing news, and we have to do everything possible to find Tempus and Olive, but it's certainly not your fault."

My brows lifted. "You're not mad at me? Not even a little bit?"

He shook his head. "Was there really anything you could have done to stop this from happening?"

I shrugged. "Maybe, I don't know. I could have…done…something."

"Jayne, what would you have done? Stop beating yourself up. I know you want everything to be perfect at the shop, but things happen." He scrubbed a hand over his face and sighed. "Granted, not usually things that put the whole world at risk."

I wasn't getting fired, but I wasn't exactly filled with glee. Sanders and Olive were still in danger. "There are tons of people working on this, Dad. And tons of resources."

"I would expect nothing less from the Ellinghams. But I'm coming down there. This is a company problem to some extent and I need to be there."

My phone buzzed. It was a text from Corette. I didn't want to ignore her, but I wasn't about to hang up on my dad either.

I glanced at it, reading it quickly.

Call me soon. Important.

I looked back up at my dad. "I expected you to say that. You can stay with me. I'll sleep on the couch."

He made an odd face. "That's nice, but the company suite will have more room."

"I don't think you can use that apartment until the sheriff gives the all clear. Technically, it's part of an ongoing investigation."

My father rubbed his forehead. "Right." Then he smiled tightly. "It will be nice to see you. These aren't the circumstances under which I'd hoped to be visiting, but it will be nice, nonetheless."

"Will Mom come with you? Or Uncle Kris?"

"No. You don't have the room for us and bringing your uncle would only create more havoc, I'm sure."

"Yeah, probably." Having Santa Claus suddenly show up in town wasn't going to help things. "Thanks for understanding and not being mad. I really am sorry."

"I know. And I'm sorry you have to deal with this. See you tomorrow night. Love you."

"Tomorrow. Love you."

The snow stilled. I whipped out my phone and punched up Corette's shop number.

"Ever After Bridal Boutique, Corette speaking."

"Corette, it's Jayne. I got your text."

"Good, good. I may have something that could help you. Well, help your *situation*. Can you come by the shop?"

"I can be there in fifteen minutes. Maybe less."

"Perfect."

I tucked my phone into my purse, slung it across my body, then locked up my office. In the warehouse, I grabbed one of the shop bikes kept for employee use, wheeled it outside and hit the road.

Thirteen minutes later, I was walking into Ever After. A little sweatier than I would have liked, but this wasn't the time to be picky about such things.

Corette greeted me at the door and ushered me

back to her office.

As soon as she shut the door, I had to ask, "What's up?"

She sat at her desk, her expression tentative. "After my daughters and I did the spell for you against nightmares, we had a long talk about…the possibilities. Our talk led to us to believe that there was potentially more at stake than we'd originally realized. Marigold scryed into the future—now, that's not an exact magic and it's very draining for her, but she's very good at it—anyway, what she saw was grim, to say the least."

"Death?" My voice was hoarse with nerves. "Because that's what Jacque Baptiste saw."

"I've never known him to be wrong." Her smile was thin and didn't reach her eyes.

"Are you saying Marigold saw death too?"

"Yes."

I groaned and covered my face with my hands. This was horrible news. "Sanders is dead, isn't he?"

"I don't know. I certainly hope not, but that's not what I called you here to tell you."

I dropped my hands. "It's not?"

"No. When my daughters and I realized what *might* happen, we decided to take action."

"You did? What kind of action?" That was a dumb question. Obviously it was something witchy. What else?

"We called in all the witches we trusted and cast the largest spell we've ever cast."

I was right. Something witchy. A bright spark lit inside me, the same feeling I got when I saw the first snowfall of the year. I was almost breathless with anticipation. "What kind of spell? Who did you cast it on?"

"Not on a person. The town. We cast a spell over the entire vicinity of Nocturne Falls. And it wasn't a spell so much as a preventative incantation, really."

"What does this incantation prevent?"

"Anyone with evil in their heart or who has committed an evil deed from leaving the boundaries of Nocturne Falls. Nor will it allow their black magic to penetrate beyond the town's borders."

Nervous energy pushed me to my feet. I paced to the back wall and returned as I translated what she'd said. "Are you telling me that Luna is trapped in Nocturne Falls? That she's somewhere in town with Tempus and Olive unable to leave?"

Corette smiled much more brightly this time. "That's exactly what I'm telling you. I'm sorry I didn't contact you earlier, but I only just heard what had happened."

"Is this also why only those of us in town were affected by the strange sleep issues?"

"Most likely. If Luna was doing that deliberately, it was with evil intent. So our spell would have contained it to town."

New hope sprang up inside me. "Oh, this is excellent. It's amazing. It's perfect. Thank you. I owe you big time, big, huge. Anything you want or need or—do you want to become a baroness? I think I can arrange that. It would be linked to a barony in the North Pole, but it's still a royal title and—"

She laughed. "None of that is necessary, but

there's one more thing I have to tell you. The spell only lasts a day. And because it's such strong magic, Luna can probably feel its ebb and flow. Which means…" She glanced at the delicate gold-and-diamond timepiece on her wrist and her smile disappeared. "In two hours, Luna Nyx will be free to leave. And she knows it."

Juggling my phone while pushing the bike down the sidewalk wasn't easy, but I managed. Adrenalin, probably.

Birdie answered two rings in. "Hello?"

I was almost out of breath with the excitement of it all but I had to get things moving, so I'd called the one person I could rely on to spread the news to everyone who needed to know. "Birdie, listen, this is very important."

"I'm all ears. That's a werewolf joke. Sorry, this is serious. Listening."

I rolled my eyes but only briefly as I didn't want to accidentally run the bike into a lamp post. "Long story short. Luna is still in town. The witches cast a spell to keep her here but it's only going to last two more hours and Corette thinks there's a good chance Luna can feel the spell's power waning, so you've got to get everyone organized and searching immediately."

"For real? Well, shut my mouth. How about that. I'll get right on it."

"Great, thank you. I'm headed back to the shop, but I'll be available to help as soon as I make sure everything's all right there."

"Maybe you ought to stay there, Princess. I mean, Luna's a tough customer, being a reaper and all, and we wouldn't want you to—"

"Don't even try it, Birdie. I'm helping. Did Greyson and the sheriff go see Lucien?"

"They left for his place about five minutes ago. I imagine they're just about arriving."

"Okay, I'll text Greyson and let him know and you text the sheriff, then maybe they can talk Lucien into being a little more cooperative."

She snorted. "I doubt that."

So did I. "Where's Cooper?"

She sighed. "The kitchen fire turned out to be a false alarm. Someone left a tray of biscuits in the oven so it was a lot of smoke but not much else. However, right after that call, they got another one. A tourist drove their car into the lake. I imagine Cooper will be there a while until they get that poor sap out of the drink."

"I suppose so. Well, I'll text him too."

"All right, I'll get on the horn and let the rest of the crew know."

"Thanks, Birdie."

"You betcha."

I hung up and did something I'd never done before: I group texted Cooper and Greyson. I wasn't sure how they were going to feel about that, but time was everything right now.

Witches cast a spell to keep Luna here. Search parties

forming. Headed to the shop then I'll be searching too. No need to respond I know you're busy.

I slipped the phone in my purse and jumped back on the bike, pedaling like mad to get home. I wheeled it into the warehouse, propped it on the stand with the rest, and went into the store. Juniper and Kip were both leaning on the counter looking half-dead.

Normally, the leaning thing would have earned them a very boss-like look of reproach, but today they got a pass.

They straightened when they saw me anyway.

I stopped in front of the counter. "Hey, how's it going? Kind of slow, huh? Which is good."

They both nodded. Kip barely stifled a yawn and started moving toward the shelves. "I'll go do a walk through."

"Thanks," Juniper said. Then she looked at me. "How are you doing?"

"A little better." I told her about Corette's news.

That woke her up. "That's great."

"It is."

"What are you going to do?"

"Change and figure out where to start looking."

She smiled. "Then get moving. And good luck."

"Thanks." I raced upstairs to my apartment. I shucked my work clothes in favor of jeans, T-shirt, and hoodie (and ditched the sensible heels for truly sensible ballet flats), and was about to return to the warehouse when I saw the snow in the globe on my side table going at full tilt.

I closed my eyes for a minute. This couldn't be good. I steeled myself for whatever was about to happen and pressed the button to answer.

My dad's face appeared, and before he could speak, I launched a pre-emptive strike. "I'm glad you called back, I have great news. Luna is still in town." I explained what the witches had done. It seemed to catch him off guard. "So what did you call about?"

"I was going to tell you that your uncle had decided to come after all, but in the light of this news…maybe that won't be necessary."

"Whatever you think." I didn't want to tell my dad that neither of them needed to come, but that would be the simplest outcome. For me, anyway. Having either of them here would make things substantially more complicated and when this was over, my staff and I were going to need a couple of easy days so we could catch our breath. And catch up on our sleep. "If you want to see what happens today, I can call you the minute she's found. Or not."

He nodded slowly. "All right. Let's do that. I'll tell your uncle to cool his jets. Literally. He had the sleigh fired up."

Wow, talk about the nick of time. No pun intended. "Any advice on where Luna might have hidden away? Seeing as how you're part elemental and all."

He snorted. "But I'm not a reaper. That's a mindset I don't really relate to. I'm sure she'll turn up, though. Nocturne Falls isn't exactly New York City. There are only so many places to hide."

"Right." I thought for a second. "Where would you hide if you were on the run?"

A soft laugh trailed out of him. "That's easy. Somewhere cold. An ice house, a deep freeze, cold storage—anywhere I'd be comfortable but those chasing me wouldn't be."

"Makes sense." I smiled and meant it. "Thanks, Dad. Talk to you soon."

"Very soon. And Jayne, be careful." Then he winked at me and was gone.

I put the globe back on the side table, gave Spider a little scratch on the head (he was zonked out on the couch, the lucky duck), and returned to the warehouse, my phone tucked in my back pocket.

By now, I was sure the rest of the deputies and the Ellinghams and whoever else had joined the search were probably well on their way. I guess that left me as a search party of one. At least until Greyson or Cooper responded, which they hadn't yet. I sauntered out of the warehouse and stood on the sidewalk. I was filled with determination and hope. I didn't want to waste that. So if I had to be on my own for a few minutes, that was fine. I just had to figure out which way to go.

Deputy Lafitte said he'd seen Sanders and Olive headed toward the Black Rose. That was as good a place to start as anywhere else. I walked in that direction, paying attention to everything around me. There could be a clue anywhere.

Okay, maybe not, but anything was possible, right? I had great faith in Olive. Not only was she the kind of person to leave a trail if possible, but that belief gave me something to cling to. Especially with time ticking away.

As I approached the Black Rose, I slowed. This was sort of the end of my run. I picked my way around the inn, looking at everything as I went. But I found nothing. Disappointment started to set in.

What if this wasn't where they'd stopped? What if their final destination was in this direction, but not here?

I started walking again, eyes open and mind receptive. But the neighborhood was pretty quiet and there was nothing along the way to make me think Olive had been able to leave any breadcrumbs behind. *If* she and Sanders had actually continued this way.

I kept moving, my mind drifting as I tried to imagine where Luna might have gone. She didn't know the town—unless she'd been here before to suss things out and come up with a plan B if her plan A didn't work out. Which seemed like it might be the case.

Even worse, Halloween was only a few weeks behind us and in this town, no one, supernatural or human, would have looked at her twice. She could have blended right in, done her recon, and been gone with no one the wiser.

So what would she have found? What kind of place would she have looked at and thought, 'yep, that's my potential hideout'?

The one place that kept popping up in my head was Insomnia, Lucien's nightclub. I mean, the irony was sort of perfect. Would he aid her? I really didn't think so, but I didn't know the man. And he certainly hadn't given off the kind of warm fuzzies that made me instantly want to defend him. He was a reaper. Maybe they stuck together. And maybe they didn't.

But right now, that was all I could come up with.

The street ended at another cross street and I

found myself at the library. Now that was coming full circle. I walked over and sat on the wide stone steps. The rest was nice, even if it was just for a minute. I pulled out my phone to see if Cooper or Greyson had texted me back yet. I hadn't felt the phone vibrate, but then I'd been occupied. If they had texted, I was going to tell them I was on my way to Insomnia. I might as well have a look around over there. And while I was waiting for the Ryde service to pick me up, I'd call Birdie and see if anyone else had found anything yet.

And, I guess, tell her that I hadn't.

I stared at my phone. No texts from anyone. But my screen wallpaper was a picture of Spider I'd taken on the night of Halloween. I'd been invited to the Black and Orange Ball, the biggest party in Nocturne Falls, but choosing between Cooper and Greyson had been impossible, so I'd opted to work in the store that night, handing out candy to all the trick-or-treaters who came in.

Because they were awesome and understanding guys, Greyson and Cooper had both sent me gifts of chocolates from Delaney's Delectables. Her Halloween special, in fact: a coffin-shaped box filled with dark chocolate truffles. The perfect treat for that occasion, and it had come wrapped in a black ribbon patterned with smiling white skulls.

When I'd closed up the shop and gone home, I'd made a bow out of the two ribbons and tied it around Spider's neck. Then I'd taken his picture. After I told him how handsome he looked, I swear he posed.

I smiled at the picture now, staring at those skulls and thinking about my dad's words. I lifted my head to watch a car go by, and as I followed it down the road, my gaze came to land on the building next to the library.

The old funeral home.

Jacque and Marigold had both seen death. Was this what they'd seen? I couldn't take my eyes off the building. And the longer I looked, the more I wondered.

Had Luna seen it too?

A tremor rippled through me, the sort of feeling you get when you realize something ahead of everyone else.

I was on my feet and walking toward the place before I even knew what I was doing. The landscaping around it was overgrown, giving me easy cover. I ducked through the hedges along the edge of the parking lot and crouched down.

The place was empty and would be for a while longer, I supposed. According to Birdie, it was stuck in probate because the owner had passed without a will. Kinda funny, when you consider his line of work and that he really should have known better.

If Luna was in there, she certainly wouldn't be using the front door. I crept around toward the back, but only as far as the corner. From there I could see two entrances. One right in the back, a set of fancy double doors with a slight ramp. Probably for taking the casket out. And another single door, set off to the side. It was a simple door with a heavy duty lock.

Everything about the building looked abandoned and untouched—except for the lock on that door. It had several scrapes on it that had left bright streaks behind on the tarnished metal.

Like it had been freshly, and somewhat ineptly, picked.

I was breathing open-mouthed now, almost hyperventilating. She was here. She had to be. Where else could she be? And where else would a reaper feel more at home than a funeral parlor?

I'd done it. I'd figured it out.

At least I thought I had. I mean, it had just been Halloween. Was it possible that the marks on that lock were the results of kids fooling around? Daring each other to spend five minutes in the place? I could see that too.

I had to get closer and see if Sanders was in there. What I needed was Greyson's ability to hear heartbeats.

Or, you know, Greyson himself.

I checked my phone again to see if he'd answered my earlier text yet, even though I knew he hadn't. Nope. I sent him and Cooper another joint message. *Where are you guys? I could use some backup.*

Either one of them would be helpful right now. Maybe I should call Birdie, but I was a little worried about her turning a possibility into a full-blown event and having the entire fleet of Nocturne Falls first responders show up, sirens blaring and lights flashing.

I could only imagine what kind of reaction Luna might have to that. If Sanders and Olive were still alive—and I really, really hoped they were—I didn't want to do anything to jeopardize their chances of staying that way.

I looked at my phone again to check the time. Barely an hour before she was free to waltz right out of town.

The only way I could find out if she or Sanders or Olive were in there was to get in there myself. But going into that building alone was stupid and dangerous, and I knew that.

Instead, I crept further toward the back, hoping I'd see something that might confirm my suspicions. But there wasn't anything else. I sighed and leaned against the trunk of a pine at the corner of the property.

What had I expected? A getaway car? Luna's big black SUV? Parking that behind the funeral home would not have gone unnoticed.

I stared over at the library parking lot. There were *three* big black SUVs there. That kind of vehicle was pretty common. Heck, even Marigold drove one. Could Luna have parked there in plain sight?

Son of a nutcracker, she absolutely could have. I could be looking at her car right now.

I had to go in. I didn't have a choice. And the longer I thought about it, the more likely I was to chicken out. I'd be quick. I had the advantage of the

Saint Nick Slide, after all. I'd slip in, confirm Sanders and Olive were in there, then slip right back out and get help.

In fact, I'd go one better. I'd send Greyson and Cooper another text, telling them what I was about to do. That way, if things didn't go as planned, at least they'd know where to find me. Or my body.

That was a happy thought.

I hoped one of them would take care of Spider. Or maybe Juni would take him. She loved Spider. My poor motherless baby.

Okay, I was getting ahead of myself. Let's not be dead yet.

I pulled out my phone and started typing. *At the old funeral home, pretty sure Luna is here. Going in to check. Come soon as you can.*

If that didn't get them moving, I didn't know what would. I put the phone back in my pocket, looked both ways (not a soul in sight), and dashed forward toward the plain door. A second later, thanks to my magical abilities, I was inside.

And perched precariously on the edge of a landing. I wobbled forward, catching the railing in time to keep myself from pitching down the steep set of stairs in front of me. Snowballs. Tumbling down the steps would not be good. For me or for being stealthy.

My dizzy eyes struggled to focus, but it was dark and there wasn't much to see. I slid my hand off the railing where it ended and felt around on the interior wall. I found and avoided a light switch, then a doorknob. My head was almost back to normal and my eyes had adjusted enough that I could make out the door beside me. It must lead to the inside of the funeral home.

I wondered if it smelled as bad as this stairwell did. I hoped not. The place reeked with the antiseptic tang of a hospital on steroids. I wrinkled my nose and tried to breathe through my mouth. I could imagine what that stink was from: the chemicals it took to clean up all the deceased juices. Ew. I immediately wished I hadn't thought that.

I was getting a little queasy. Great. This was a fine time to live up to the delicate sensibilities of being a princess.

I pulled my T-shirt up over my nose and let it filter out the smell while I listened. I didn't hear much at first.

Then a soft, almost wheezy sound reached my ears. Breathing? There was no way that would be happening in a funeral home unless someone was in here.

The dizziness was gone now, so I started down the steps, thankful my ballet flats had rubber soles. As long as I was careful and slow, I was soundless. I kept my hand on the railing and went as far as where the wall stopped and the stairs opened onto the basement.

There I crouched down and snuck a peek between the bannisters.

Sanders was strapped to a stainless steel table that looked very much like it might have been used for something really gross when this place was operational. It seemed like he was unconscious, or maybe Luna had used the hourglass to put him to sleep. Either way, I knew he was breathing—I could hear him and see his chest rise and fall. That was a good thing.

There was no sign of Olive though, and that worried me.

I went down another stair so I could see more of the room. The whole thing was tiled in white and there was a drain in the floor, which I really didn't want to think about. There were no windows. I guess it wasn't the kind of operation you wanted people to be able to peek in on. The only light came from a digital clock on the counter. For elf eyes, it was enough.

Caskets were stacked up against the far wall, but the two walls closest to me had glass-front cabinets and countertops that held clear jugs of fluid, stainless steel instruments, and boxes of all sorts of things. Part of the counter was a desk area with a wheeled office chair tucked under it. A layer of dust draped everything.

I straightened. No point in crouching anymore. I walked down until I was on the ground floor. I had to find Olive. I needed to know she was okay, or at least that she was here. Maybe I should try to wake Sanders up and see if he knew where she was.

I started toward him but a small sound stopped me in my tracks. It was the soft snick of metal. Then another sound followed it. The muted squeal of unused hinges.

Someone had just opened the door on the landing.

The lights came on next, showing off the room in all its awful, morbid glory, but all I could think about was hiding. And the only place that made sense was one of the caskets. The one in the corner on the floor looked like the easiest to get into since it wouldn't require any climbing. I grabbed a rubber glove off the counter as I went past, and as I climbed in, I wadded the glove up and stuck it between the lid and the box.

It made enough of a space that I could see out with one eye and, more importantly, breathe. The sightline only showed me the bottom two steps. I lay still, trying to calm my pounding pulse. If reapers could hear heartbeats the way vampires could, I was in deep frost.

Black lace-up ankle boots were the first things I saw.

Luna.

My teeth ground together. I knew it. Her time as a reaper of the criminally insane had really done a number on her. And now I was freaking stuck here until Greyson and Cooper showed up. They had better show up fast. If I died because they were late to the scene, I was done dating both of them.

Ignore that. Panic talking.

A second set of shoes came into view. Sensible brown loafers.

Olive. She was alive!

A new urgency struck me. Was Luna planning to off Olive right before she left town with Sanders? If that was her plan, there was no way I could stay hidden. I'd have to leap out and use the element of surprise to catch her off guard and keep her from hurting—

"Sit down and shut up."

I blinked, trying to make sense of what I'd just heard. It wasn't the words that boggled me, but the fact that they'd been said in Olive's voice. That didn't compute.

The black boots moved toward the chair, but the loafers stayed put. The chair rolled out from under the counter and the owner of those boots sat. "You think you can replace me? You can't."

That was definitely Luna's voice.

Olive's voice again, this time laughing. "I already have."

Whoa. *Whoa*. What was going on here?

"We had a deal," Luna said. "You gave me your word."

More laughing from Olive. "The fact that you believed me just shows how stupid you are."

A low growl filled the space. I guess it was coming out of Luna. "I could kill you with the touch of my hand."

Yep, Luna. And yelping yetis, Olive hadn't been kidnapped at all, by the sound of things. She was in on this! I didn't even know what to do with that.

The response to Luna's growl was a soft rattle. Like something being shaken.

Olive spoke again. "You want this hourglass back in one piece or should I drop it now?"

"You wouldn't dare."

"Yes," Olive said. "I would. And let me remind you that your touch won't work on me. I'm an elemental just like you, remember?"

I almost gasped. I don't know which was more surprising—that Olive was an elemental or that a reaper's touch wouldn't work on another elemental. Why hadn't Lucien told me that? Maybe that only applied to full-blooded elementals. Or maybe Lucien had purposefully held back that info? That seemed more reasonable.

Luna hissed. "Sanders never should have told you that. That wasn't his secret to tell."

"He wanted me to feel safer around you. Like that was suddenly going to make us best friends." Olive snorted. "You never should have come back. He was supposed to love me the way I love him, but you turned him against me."

Olive loved Sanders? This was seriously messing with my head.

"He never would have loved you," Luna said.

Oh, Luna. Don't poke the crazy.

"I don't care anymore." Olive sounded like she was barely keeping it together. "If we can't be together, then it's time for me to take my rightful place as the new Sandman."

Oh boy. Olive's crazy went deeper than I imagined.

Luna's feet moved, pushing the chair back a little. "Being the Sandman is all he's ever known. What else is he supposed to do?"

"What do I care? As soon as we can get out of this town, he's your problem. The last thing I'm going to do for you is put the town to sleep again so we can all leave safely, but I'm only doing that because I never want to see either of you again."

"And you'll give me my hourglass back?"

"Yes. Unless you try something stupid again. Then I promise you, I will shatter it to dust."

Huh. I wonder what Luna had tried. And how Olive got to be so insane. I guess that high school counseling hadn't done the trick after all.

The air was getting stale in the casket. Also, my attempts at pretending I wasn't in a casket were starting to fail. I wanted out. Bad. I really needed my guys to show up.

Then, in a case of the worst timing ever, my phone vibrated.

Big hairy snowballs.

I squirmed around trying to reach it but the noise seemed amplified in the small space. There was no way they hadn't heard it.

"What was that?" Olive said.

Maybe she'd think it was Sanders snoring. I turned the phone to silent, then checked the message. Greyson and Cooper were on their way.

Please let them get here in time. And not just to collect my remains.

Feet shuffled toward me but I didn't have time to see who it was as I stuffed the phone back in my pocket. I reached for the lid's lining, figuring that would give me something to hold onto and keep it shut if someone tried to open it.

But I was too late.

Luna peered down at me and squinted. "You."

"Hi." Dumbest response ever, but it was out of my mouth now. "Listen, I'll just—"

"What are you doing here?" Olive glared at me. The glasses were gone, but otherwise, she pretty much looked the same. Sanders' hourglass hung around her waist on the same cord he'd used, and Luna's nightmare glass was in Olive's hand. So that was new.

I climbed out. At least I wasn't in the casket anymore. "Looking for you and Sanders. I thought Luna had kidnapped you both."

Olive smiled. "Sounds about right." She jerked her head at Luna. "Scare her into a coma."

"I can't," Luna said. "She's got magic to prevent that." She narrowed her eyes at me. "You went to the witches, didn't you?"

"Yep. And that's why you can't leave town, too." I shot Olive a look. "Either of you. Because you have evil in your hearts."

Olive rolled her eyes. "Oh, shut up, Princess Perfect, or I'll have Luna do what she does best and off you."

"Off me?" I put my hands on my hips in a show of confidence I wasn't totally feeling. "First of all, who talks like that? And secondly, don't waste your breath. I've got enough elemental blood running through my veins to make that impossible." Maybe I did, maybe I didn't, but it was a good bluff. Although one I hoped not to test.

That shut Olive up for a second. Luna looked at me with new interest.

Good, because I was on a roll now. "Not only that, I am still the Winter Princess which means—" I raised my hands to freeze them both in place.

Luna took a swing at me. I don't know if it was my elfy quickness or my nerves being trigger-thin, but I dodged enough that her fist whistled through my hair.

I scrambled sideways, putting Sanders between us. Turns out, the embalming table he was strapped to was on wheels. Made it easy to use him as a shield, which wasn't the nicest thing in the world to do, but I felt confident Luna wouldn't hurt him.

Also, he was still unconscious, so maybe he'd never know.

Olive shook her head. "We'll figure something out, because we can't let you live, sorry. Our future depends on no witnesses." She pointed at Luna. "You take that side."

Luna nodded.

Then they both moved toward me. The ceiling was too low to jump and I wasn't sure I could climb over Sanders. Those stupid daytime pajamas were slippery satin and he was the size of a mountain. It would be like climbing an enormous, greased bean bag.

A door opened upstairs and a split-second later, Greyson appeared. His vampire speed had allowed him to descend the stairs without being seen or making a sound. "Cooper's on his way," he yelled as he grabbed Olive.

That distraction was all I needed. I lunged for Luna and snagged the scythe off her belt.

Everything changed the moment my fingers wrapped around the hilt of the scythe. It was like an x-ray filter dropped over my eyes and I could see people's souls. I mean, I could still see who they were. Olive looked like Olive and Sanders looked like Sanders, but they were also more than that. They'd become creatures of light and dark.

And in Greyson's case, a creature of gray nothingness.

Where everyone else wore an aura of light around them that faded to black at the edges, Greyson looked…smudged. Where the aura should have been was a wavering grayness. Some kind of supernatural fog. I supposed it was because he was technically dead already.

Sanders glow had a thin edge of black, but Olive's was almost entirely dark. I knew instinctively that this wasn't just an aura, it was a measure of their lives. Olive wasn't a good person.

I looked at Luna, expecting not to see anything

around her either since Greyson had told me at the party that she didn't register, but I could see her aura plain as day. Her line of black was substantially thicker than Sanders but nowhere near Olive's. She was staring at me with a lost expression. She held her hands up. "Please don't kill me. And please don't hurt Tempus."

I lifted the scythe. "Stay back and I won't."

Olive was still struggling against Greyson, throwing elbows and trying to stomp on his feet.

I pointed a hand at her and froze her feet to the ground, then I froze her arms to her body. It was tricky to manage that without sealing her and Greyson together, but I did it. I had to. I couldn't have her dropping Luna's nightmare glass.

Olive yowled in frustration as she tried to move. "How dare you? I'm the Sandman now. You can't do that to—"

I gagged her with a snowball. "Olive, it's over."

Cooper came charging down the steps. "The sheriff and deputies are right behind me." He made a face at Olive, then looked at me. "Why is she frozen up?"

He was all bright light. But then I wouldn't have expected anything less. I turned toward Luna. "Would you like to explain?"

She nodded, the most subdued I'd seen her. "It started innocently enough. I was going to kidnap Tempus—"

Cooper snorted. "You have a warped definition of innocent."

She shook her head. "That's not really how I meant it. If things went well between us here, I was going to surprise him with a trip. Just the two of us. Like old times." She stared at her hands. "I've missed him so much."

She cleared her throat and looked up again. "Olive was helping me. Or at least, I thought she was. Last night, right before I was supposed to meet Tempus for dinner, she called and said Tempus wanted me to meet him at the library. That he had a surprise for me. I couldn't imagine what, but I went."

Noises came out of Olive, muted by the snowball she was munching on. I shot her a look. "You'll get your chance to speak, but this isn't it." That would come later. When she was at the police station.

"When I arrived at the library, Tempus and Olive were waiting for me in the parking lot. I realized too late that Tempus was sleepwalking and Olive was controlling him with his own hourglass. She'd stolen it from him. Before I could do anything, she used it to knock me out as well."

Her gaze shifted to Olive, darkening as she glowered at the other woman. "I woke up here. Upstairs." A muscle in her jaw twitched. "She had me locked in one of the display caskets. I made so much noise she had to let me out."

The snowball had melted enough that Olive spit it out. "She tried to kill me."

Luna's glare intensified. "I tried to take our hourglasses back."

"And then you would have killed me."

"You know that's not possible." Luna looked at me again. "I told her I'd do whatever she wanted if she'd prove to me that Tempus wasn't harmed. That's when she brought me down here."

"There was never going to be any trip," Olive said. "That was all a big story to get you on her side. She wanted Tempus to pay for rejecting her."

"Liar," Luna spat.

Olive's brows rose, her expression haughty. "Why would I care what you did to him? I've had enough of him bossing me around and taking me for granted. Do you know how much work I do for him? Everything. Every. Thing."

I let her talk, mostly because she was digging her own hole and I hadn't even needed to give her a shovel.

"He couldn't decide what to wear without me." She pulled at the ice on her arms, but it wasn't going anywhere. "All those years of being his assistant taught me one very important lesson: If I was going to do all the work, I should be the one getting all the glory."

I nodded. "So you decided you'd take over as Sandman."

"Exactly."

Cooper leaned on the counter. "How about that. I never figured the meek little assistant for the criminal mastermind."

"Me, either," Greyson said. "But the quiet ones always surprise you."

Cooper smiled. "Guess we don't have to worry about Jayne then."

Sirens echoed down from the outside.

"All right, party's over." And I was done using this scythe to keep Luna at bay. It was disconcerting seeing into people's souls like this. "Coop, you'd better do your paramedic thing with Sanders. See if you can bring him around."

"Just put his hourglass in his hand," Luna said quietly. "Once it's in his control again, it can't be used against him. And the townspeople will be able to sleep."

"Are you saying Olive is the one who created all that havoc?"

"I am. She told me upstairs everything she'd done." She slanted her eyes at Olive. "Sleep is a precious thing. Not a weapon."

I started to put the scythe down, then hesitated. "Tell me the truth. Are you the one who gave Cooper and me nightmares?"

She shook her head. "That was Olive again."

"How?"

"Sands from Tempus' hourglass can be turned into nightmares with improper handling. It's another reason the hourglass must be protected and kept out of the wrong hands."

I looked at Olive. "Is that true?"

Her lip curled back. "And what if it is? I can't help it that your boyfriend caught one."

"I suppose you planted the evidence at the apartment too, trying to make it look like Luna had been there."

A wicked smile bent her mouth. "I have no idea what you're talking about."

The blackness in her aura expanded a little more. That was really all I needed to know. "Cooper, if you would."

"Sure." He untied the hourglass from Olive's waist and brought it to the table, nestling it in Sanders' big hand.

Sanders took a deep, shuddering breath and opened his eyes. "That was some nap." He sat up. "What's going on here?"

Sheriff Merrow came down the steps with Chief Merrow behind him. I'd never been happier to see werewolves in my life.

I clapped Sanders on the shoulder. "It's quite a story."

It was good to be friendly with the people in charge. It meant that after giving my statement, I got to go home. It probably helped, too, that I told them my father was waiting to hear what had happened so he knew whether or not to come down here. No one really wanted an angry Jack Frost to show up in Nocturne Falls.

Big freezes had a way of ruining the tourist industry.

I strolled through my apartment door and took a deep breath. I was happy. About a lot of things.

Spider came running out from the bedroom, meowing at me. I grabbed him up and hugged him. "How are ya, babycat?"

He butted his head against my chin. "Mama home. Spider happy."

"Me, too." I kissed his neck. "For all kinds of reasons. I get to sleep tonight, for one." And Sanders was safe. That was the big one. "Are you hungry?"

He straightened in my arms, pushing back with

his front legs so he could look me in the eyes. "Treats? Spider loves treats."

"Shocking." I kissed his nose. "Yes, treats. Come on." I put him down and he pranced along beside me as I walked into the kitchen and pried off the top of the treat container. I sprinkled a handful on the floor.

While he hoovered those down, I went into the living room and flopped on the couch. I could have gone to sleep right then, but my day was far from over.

Instead, I picked up the globe and gave it a shake.

My dad appeared almost instantly, so it was safe to assume he'd been standing by. "So? What's the word?"

"The word is Sanders is fine. He never left town, actually. And never really knew what was going on." I told my dad the whole tale, answering his questions and assuring him all was now well.

He was visibly relieved. "That had a better outcome than I expected, but I must say, the whole thing with Olive surprises me."

"Me, too. I was going to tell you that if she ever left Sanders, I wanted to hire her here. Can you imagine what a nightmare that would have been? No pun intended."

He shook his head. "She hid being an elemental well."

I shrugged. "It's not hard to do. Hey, did you know that reapers can't take the souls of elementals?"

"Can't say that I did. Your uncle might, though. I'll have to ask him."

"Speaking of Uncle Kris, I guess you guys aren't

coming now that everything's right side up again?"

"No, we won't be making the trip. With Christmas just around the corner, we have more than enough to do."

"I can imagine." Christmas was in production all year long in the North Pole, but it got cranked up to eleven in November.

"Your mom and I will definitely come for a visit in the New Year, though."

I smiled. "I'll have the apartment ready for you."

"We miss you, Jay. But we're also very proud of the job you're doing. I know you doubt yourself, but you shouldn't. Look how you took care of this problem. You're more capable than you think, sweetheart."

"Thanks." His words were making me blush a little, but they were so good to hear. "I just want to make you guys proud."

"We know. And you do. Love you, honey."

"Love you. And Mom. Tell her I said so and that I'll call her tomorrow."

"Will do. Now get some sleep."

I laughed. "I will. Bye."

"Bye." He hung up and the snow settled.

I put the globe back on the table. As much as I wanted to crash, I really couldn't. My team was just as tired as I was and we had a store to run. I needed to go back downstairs and see what I could do to help us all get through the rest of the day.

That meant putting my work clothes back on. I groaned.

Spider trotted toward me, jumped up on the coffee

table, and started to clean his face.

I watched him for a moment. "You have the life, you know that?"

"Spider has good mama."

I smiled at him and shook my head. "Sweet talker."

I got up and went to the bedroom to change. I couldn't bring myself to get back into the outfit I'd had on before, so I went with jeans, boots and a sweater. Cute and casual, but still dressed up enough for retail. And once I put a store apron on over it, I'd be as dressed up as anyone else.

The store was busier than it had been earlier so I'd arrived at the right time. Turned out just to be a short rush. Once that was over, we had enough of a break that I could fill Kip and Juniper in on the whole ordeal.

Eyes round, Juniper shook her head. "Olive Pine. Who would have guessed?"

"I know, right?"

Kip yawned. "Crazy."

Poor guy still looked on the verge of collapse. "Kip, why don't you knock off and go get some sleep? I can handle the rest of your shift."

He blinked hard. "Oh no, I'm fine."

Juniper laughed. "No, you're not. Go home."

He looked a little embarrassed, but grateful. "You're sure?"

"Yep. Go."

"Thank you." He whipped off his apron, folded it up, and disappeared.

Juniper planted her hands on the counter and

leaned on them. "That was nice of you."

"I was afraid he'd stroke out if he didn't get some sleep soon."

She laughed. "That would be worse." Then her smile turned wistful. "This is nice, you and me here. Like when you first arrived."

I nodded. "We should have some chocolate to celebrate."

Half an hour later, with a serious dent in the candy stash under the counter, we were doing all right. Tired, but a little boosted by the sugar and the fun of working together again. The bells over the door rang and Cooper and Greyson walked in.

It was weird but nice to see them together. I was glad they could share the same air space without hurling insults or having some kind of testosterone battle. Or maybe they'd already gotten that out of the way.

I smiled at them. "What's up? Come to give me an update?"

Cooper nodded as he and Greyson stopped in front of the counter. "Something like that."

I came out from behind the counter. "All right, lay it on me."

He did. "Olive's being held in the cell reserved for supernaturals."

"The one in the Basement?" That was an employees-only secret area below the town that held storage rooms, passageways, all kinds of stuff. I also thought it would be a perfect place to retreat to if the zombie apocalypse ever happened.

"Yes," Cooper said. "Which is where you come in.

She's lived as a winter elf for so long, that they feel she should be extradited to the North Pole and tried in your courts. Sheriff Merrow needs to talk to your father about all that."

"I'll handle it first thing tomorrow, but I'm sure he'll send some of the royal guards for her."

"I'll tell the sheriff."

"Thanks." I glanced at Greyson. "And thank you for getting Olive under control."

He lifted one shoulder nonchalantly. "It was a team effort."

Cooper hooked his thumbs in his uniform belt. "Sorry I wasn't there sooner, but getting that car out of the lake took a while." He gave Greyson some side-eye. "I don't have a job I can just walk away from, like some people."

And there it was.

Greyson opened his mouth to reply, but I put my hand on his chest and laughed. "All right, let's not start anything."

The bells over the door jangled again, but the two men in front of me blocked my view.

I gave them both a stern look. "I have customers to take care of, so you two are going to have to—"

"Well, well. Am I interrupting a party?"

At the sound of that voice, Cooper and I stared at each other like we'd just heard a ghost. I put my hands on his and Greyson's shoulders and pushed them apart like curtains.

I stared at the woman who'd just walked in. After the day I'd had, I wasn't sure I could believe my eyes. Or that I wanted to. My mouth went dry, but I managed one word: "Lark?"

She laughed, throwing her head back in that way she'd always had. "Surprised to see me?"

I swallowed and found my voice, despite the storm of emotions rolling through me. "More than I can say."

The End

Want to be up to date on new books, new audiobooks & other fun stuff from me?

Sign-up for my NEWSLETTER.
No spam, just news (sales, freebies, releases, you know, all that jazz.)
http://bit.ly/1kkLgHi

If you loved the book and want to help the series grow, tell a friend about the book and take time to leave a review!

About the Author

USA Today Best Selling Author Kristen Painter is a little obsessed with cats, books, chocolate, and shoes. It's a healthy mix. She loves to entertain her readers with interesting twists and unforgettable characters. She currently writes the best-selling paranormal romance series, Nocturne Falls, and award-winning urban fantasy. The former college English teacher can often be found all over social media where she loves to interact with readers:

Website: kristenpainter.com
Twitter: @Kristen_Painter
Facebook: KristenPainterAuthor
Instagram: kristen_painter

Other books by Kristen Painter

COZY MYSTERY:

Jayne Frost series:
Miss Frost Solves A Cold Case: A Nocturne Falls
Mystery
Miss Frost Ices The Imp: A Nocturne Falls Mystery
Miss Frost Saves The Sandman: A Nocturne Falls
Mystery

PARANORMAL ROMANCE:

Nocturne Falls series:
The Vampire's Mail Order Bride
The Werewolf Meets His Match
The Gargoyle Gets His Girl
The Professor Woos The Witch
The Witch's Halloween Hero – short story
The Werewolf's Christmas Wish – short story
The Vampire's Fake Fiancée
The Vampire's Valentine Surprise – short story
The Shifter Romances The Writer
The Vampire's True Love Trials – short story

Sin City Collectors series:
Queen of Hearts
Dead Man's Hand
Double or Nothing

Standalone Paranormal Romance:
Dark Kiss of the Reaper
Heart of Fire
Recipe for Magic
Miss Bramble and the Leviathan

URBAN FANTASY:

The House of Comarré series:
Forbidden Blood
Blood Rights
Flesh and Blood
Bad Blood
Out For Blood
Last Blood

The Crescent City series:
House of the Rising Sun
City of Eternal Night
Garden of Dreams and Desires

Nothing is completed without an amazing team.

Many thanks to:
Cover design: Keri Knudson
Interior formatting: Author E.M.S
Editor: Elayne Morgan
Copyedits/proofs: Marlene Engel

Baltimore County
Public Library

Made in the USA
San Bernardino, CA
09 December 2016